# LIGHTNING STRIKES TWICE

Williemae Latimore

# LIGHTNING STRIKES TWICE

*iUniverse books may be ordered through booksellers or by contacting:*

*iUniverse*
*1663 Liberty Drive*
*Bloomington, IN 47403*
*www.iuniverse.com*
*844-349-9409*

*ISBN: 978-1-6632-2663-1 (sc)*
*ISBN: 978-1-6632-2664-8 (e)*

*Print information available on the last page.*

*iUniverse rev. date: 07/19/2021*

# CHAPTER 1

SONJA FELDER WAS A CONSCIENTIOUS NINE-YEAR-OLD LITTLE GIRL with a mind of a sixteen-year-old. She had a good idea of what she wanted out of life and what she had to do to get where she wanted to go. Because her parents divorced so early in her life, she had the responsibility to maintain control of much about her cares.

Some days, because her mother had to work, she was alone when she came home from school. Her mother had to work. Sonja's dad and mom respected each other and were friends. Her father made the choice, and her mother accepted what he felt was best for him. Twice a week, when he could, her dad would pick her up after school and bring her home after dinner.

Sonja dad, whose name was Novadec, had remarried. Him and his wife Nora had three children, ages two, three and five. Novadec got his name from around the months he was born. The birthing process started the last few minutes on the 30th day of November and completed the first few minutes of December 1st.

His parents were old and not well educated, but somewhat liberal. They chose the month closest to his birth and combined the wording to come up with a name for their third son. They named all of their children after things around them. Their daughters were named May, Jan, and Windsong. Their sons were Rivers and another, Stony. The Felders did not want their children named after anyone in particular. They wanted them to have their own identity.

Mrs. Felder's name was Mary, after a family member, and Mr. Felder was named Joseph, for someone out of the Bible. Novadec met his first wife Deloris Whitman while attending the County

1

College. They were attending many of the same classes1 at the same time. Both were Engineering students. So, on campus, they had a lot in common. Novadec's parents were farmers. His sisters and brothers took over running the farm when their aging parents could no longer. They were satisfied with their duties on the farm. All of them built or purchased homes around their parents farm, except Novadec. Each family selected a crop to zero in for the market, then they all got behind that person from the time of planting, cultivating until it was ready for the market. They formed a corporation within the family. All profits, from each crop, were split equally.

Novadec did his share for a while, but his interest lay elsewhere. His brothers had gone to college and studied Agriculture, his sisters, Business. He decided Engineering. He felt that would fit in or out of Agriculture. Novadec wanted to explore other work during the summer. He did not want to be tied down eating dust. He thought, maybe one day he may be satisfied settling there and raising a family, but after college, not right away. Novadec wanted to see how the others in the world lived.

Each Felder child had time away to further their education but were required to work on the farm any free time they had. Novadec met Deloris in college, fell madly in love, and they got married a year later. Deloris was not the farmer wife type. She liked city life. Sonja was born a year after they got married. The three of them lived in a five-room apartment with two bedrooms. It was hectic for Novadec because he was used to spacious living conditions.

Along with college, city life and family, he still had family farm responsibilities. He spent his weekends on the farm and his evenings trying to be a husband, father, and student. The last year of college was hectic for Deloris and Novadec. Novadec's mother would sometimes care for Sonja during the week because Deloris worked part time in addition to attending college. She was trying to help with the living expenses, as well as, complete her education and be a mother and wife. However, because they were young, career-oriented parents many situation got crossed up. They began to disagree on many challenging outlooks. Novadec wanted Deloris to spend the weekend with him on the farm helping. But, she wanted to spend the time cleaning up the apartment, wash clothing, shop, rest and study, as well as spend time with Sonja.

Novadec could not let his family down because the income was what kept things going. The little money Deloris brought in was nearly enough. He wanted her to give up that part-time job and use that time to do chores and so on. Then she would be able to help on the farm weekends. Just the thought of working on a farm, she wanted no part of it. She had much work full-time and fit her other responsibilities in wherever she could, which included her education.

# CHAPTER 2

NOVADEC FINISHED COLLEGE FIRST BECAUSE DELORIS HAD TO TAKE a semester off when the baby was born. Throughout college, Novadec maintains a high-grade point average so did Deloris. It was inevitable because the both of them studied together reinforcing each other and correcting mistakes of each other. Even with the problems they were having, they still studied together and reviewed one another's work. Deloris was always the one Ito type up the reports!

After completing college, Novadec got several good job offers. However, he had to decline them because one of his brothers was injured and would be unable to work for months, so he had to take over his duties, on the farm. Novadec was unhappy about this, but he could not let the family down.

He knew Deloris did not want to move from the city. His family lived right outside of town, but it was too much of a hassle to go and come every day. He would leave home late Saturday evenings and stay over because normally he would be too tired to travel back and forth daily.

Deloris would come out as often as she could. Novadec's family didn't care much for her, and they treated her like an outsider, simply because she refused to become a total part of the family farm. After the semester had ended, Deloris took two weeks vacation and spent the whole time trying to help on the farm. She worked in the packing house, in the field and she learned to drive a standard shift truck. She made deliveries to the produce market when necessary, yet nothing she did please the family because she did not make that total commitment to move.

Many times, even Novadec seem to disregard her presence. After work, he would hang out with his brothers and brother-in-laws, knowing she had only a short time to spend with him. Deloris tried to be a good wife. She gave up much of her time to be with her husband, but it wasn't enough. He wanted everything his way. One week passed, and he didn't come home or call. Each time Deloris called he was never home, or his parents would make excuses for him. This went on for some time over the past few years. When he did come home, much of that affection he had for her was no longer there. She had her suspicion but chose not to let it get the best of her. She loved her husband, but she did not want to live on that farm. She felt that she had rights, regardless of what anybody said or thought. She loved his family, and it didn't bother her that they chose not to like her because of the choices she made.

Deloris felt that Novadec could have taken the job offered by a very good company. The wages offered would have enabled them to be able to purchase a home in the city. She was making a good salary as well. What Novadec was doing on the farm, they could have hired someone else to do. He told her that he was going to give up farming. His brother has been back to work for some time now, yet he was still working on the farm. Not only working but living there and coming home at his convenience. He showed no concern for his wife and child. Deloris knew she know what love is, but she was no fool for anyone.

Without bothering to call, she decided to leave right after work, pick up Sonja and go to the farm. Because of the Friday traffic, she didn't get there until after ten that night. When she knocked on the door, Novadec's parents did not know what to do. Novadec heard the commotion, so he came out the room. Sonja ran to give her daddy a hug. Out the room stepped a woman. All four of them stood there dumbfounded. Deloris looked at Novadec, then to the other woman and then to his parents.

Tears are streaming down her cheeks, she spoke. "Sonja, come on Honey, we only came to say hi to your daddy." Sonja looked over at her mother.

"But Mommy, you said you were going to stay because you miss Daddy, and I miss him too," She turned and looked at the other woman and then to her father.

"Daddy, why is she in our room? Don't you want us to sleep with you anymore?" Deloris dried her tears for the sake of her daughter.

"Mommy," pointing to the other woman, "is she the reason we are not staying and you are crying? Daddy, that's why you didn't call us? You don't love us anymore.?" Deloris picked up her bag and took Sonja's hand and walked out the door.

The first thing that Monday morning Deloris made an appointment with a lawyer, for the purpose of filing for a divorce. Novadec called her several times to apologize. She accepted his apology for Sonja's sake but, proceed with the divorce. She agreed that he was welcome to see his daughter as often as he liked, and she could stay with him whenever she wanted, but if necessary, she would fight for total custody. Novadec did not oppose her in anything because he knew he was wrong. His family tried to pressure him into seeking full custody of Sonja, but he refused. He regretted what happened.

After the divorce, Novadec married Nora. He soon found out why his family pushed that girl off on him. He found out how much they disliked Deloris, simply because she chose to maintain her own identity and not become one of them. They talked about how Deloris tried to help; what a good job she did, and how fast she learned. But they still tried to make her feel inadequate. She would not throw herself into their way of thinking and show more love for farm life. Novadec was appalled. He never realized Deloris tried so hard to please him.

When he found out his parents were in on the scheme to just put her down, he was angry. He became reckless, careless and harsh in his dealing with the family. He was hard to get along with. He begin to drink and only slept with Nora when he was drunk. He lived at home with his parents. They tried to encourage him to get a house for his family, but he refused.

Nora was pregnant before they got married. The baby was born about six months after. Their first child was premature. They had bills going out of style, mostly because the family had not gotten the best insurance coverage. When the child was six-month-old Nora was out working on the farm. Mrs. Felder took care of the baby. Nora was sloppy, did not care how she looked or dressed. She gained a lot of weight. Novadec never took her any place. A little over a year later she was expecting again. Mrs. Felder was always complaining about how she threw things around, never cleaned up after herself. If Novadec's mother didn't care for the baby, the poor thing would die of filth. Novadec left early in the morning and never returned until late evenings and sometimes, late nights.

Sometimes he would bring Sonja to the house. She would stay for a while, and then he used her as an excuse to leave again to take her home. When he saw Deloris and how good she looked, the house was neat and clean, it brought back so many memories. What a fool he made of himself. Every time he left her he stopped by the bar on his way home. Deloris never as much as swore. She was soft spoken and loving. He could always tell when something was wrong because she would get quiet. He would hold her in his arms and kiss her until she told him what was wrong. Nora was very disrespectful. The language she used was disrespectful to the deaf, as well as, to a newborn baby. Novadec rarely took her off the farm.

The other brothers and sisters tried to get him to build his own home, but he kept putting them off, he stayed right there with his parents. They were tired of Nora and the sloppy way she carried herself and the kids.

Novadec would pick Sonja up twice a week. Sometimes he took her home with him but most times he wouldn't. Whenever he got to see Deloris, he was sure of a pleasant conversation. Deloris was always so neat. She kept herself, Sonja, and the apartment that way as well. When they were together, his clothing was always hung up and folded neatly, in the drawers.

He could pick up what he wanted to wear blind folded and come out looking good, every time. Now he is lucky if he finds a clean set of underwear if he didn't wash them himself or ask his mother. Nora didn't know the meaning of orderly.

Deloris had gotten a good job after she finished college. It had opportunities for promotions. After a few years, right after the time of her divorce, she got a much better position with the company. The job was about ten miles from where Novadec lived. She decided to purchase a home in the area, only because it was close to her job. Because of the nature of the engineering firm she worked for she got to see Novadec and many of his family members from time to time.

When she saw them, they would ask about Sonja and invite her out. Each year they would have a family reunion. Each year she would allow Sonja to go out, but this time she decided to go for the heck of it.

Sonja liked to sing. When she sang, the Felder children, her cousins, they would laugh at her. For a while, Sonja would refuse to go home with Novadec. Deloris picked up on her talents and start sending her for voice lessons. Sonja would sing in church and at school functions. She had a very high soprano voice, and most kids her age did not understand her talent, which was the reason they made fun of her.

# CHAPTER 3

Deloris loved clothing, so she and Sonja were always neatly dressed, for every occasion. Novadec's older brother Rivers always liked Deloris. He sat on the sidelines and made positive comments when his family put Deloris through the wringer. He always stood up for her regardless of what they said. He liked women who were gutsy enough to take control of their lives regardless of the outcome. No matter how they treated Deloris, she was still always kind, but Nora, he could not stand the sight of her. Rivers always addressed Deloris as "sister-in-law".

Rivers was in town picking up a few things for the farm. On his way home, he stopped by the restaurant to pick up a sandwich to eat. Before placing his order, he saw Deloris. He walked over to her table to pay his respects.

"Hey Sister-in-law, how are you? Believe me you are still looking good." "Hi Rivers, come on join me. What are you doing in this part of the world?"

"Hey, hey, Sister-in-law, I am only a few mile down the road. I might ask what are you doing so close to me.?"

"Oh, I work in these parts."

"You drive out here every day?"

"No, I bought a home out here It looks like my job is pretty secure." "Does Novy know you are so close?"

"I wrote him a note to let him know that I was moving. Sonja is at my parents for the summer, while I get everything straighten out." She said reaching into her purse for her notepad. "Will you give Novadec this? It's my address and tell him Sonja will be home in a couple weeks, then I will have her call." Handing him the note, she asked, "Why don't you sit down and eat?"

"But I am so dirty."

"So, you still have to eat." "Okay, if you say so."

They talked and ate. Deloris learned about all the problems in the family. Novadec and Nora fought all the time. They are driving his parents bananas. Just about everybody hates Nora. Their kids are rude, and she is expecting again. Novadec is sorry he ever messed up on her and so on and so on. Also, the farm was not doing well that year. A few of them had to get outside .jobs.

After lunch, Deloris went back to work and Rivers headed for home. She enjoyed his company and was a little sad for them. Novadec had always provided well for Sonja over the years. She decided that she would talk to him and let him know she was able to take full responsibility of Sonja and would release him from any financial responsibility, since things were not going well.

Deloris picked Sonja up from her parents a few days early so she could go to the Felder's family reunion. She got along well with most of the family now that she wasn't expected to be a part of any activities or functions within the Felder enterprise. She was respected as an outsider. Sonja was no different; she too was much the outsider. While visiting the family, she never get involved in the mudslinging games, play ball in the hot sun or play with the chickens and pigs. She spent most of her time with her grandparents helping with whatever she could, or just watching what they were doing. Novadec liked having her around sometimes because she was quite intelligent. She would read to them, sing to them and talk about what she learned in school and voice classes. They in turn would question all aspects of her life with Deloris.

Deloris and Sonja arrived early that afternoon. As soon as Sonja caught sight of her father and he her, she ran to give him a big hug, and he was waiting for it. She hadn't seen him for almost two months. She loved her father very much, and he was nuts about his little girl. Novadec wished, many times, he had not been so foolish.

He realized now that Deloris did not belong on a farm, especially if she had to turn out as hard as his sisters and present wife, Nora. He also realized that he and Nora would not be together much longer. He could not put up with her ways any longer. She did not fit into his crowd, anywhere.

He was a shame to take her out. She was nothing like he and Deloris were. With Deloris, he could take her anywhere, anytime, and she stood out. She had charm and still does. Even when she was carrying Sonja, she showed a certain commanding elegant. Always neat and made him feel like a man. She never curse or swore at him. As for drinking alcohol, when they went out she never overdid it. She may or may not take one drink. If she objected, to anything he said or did, she would let him know it a kind way. If a problem arose, he would be the only one arguing. Deloris would go in another room and leave him to argue with the four walls. He would soon discover he had no listeners, and he was being ridiculous, then he would claim his wife with hugs and kisses. Novadec yearned for that life again with Deloris.

As Novadec watched his daughter run to him, he remembered the love shared with Deloris that brought her life. He will never forget the hurt on Deloris's face when she caught him with Nora. He never loved Nora. He used her to get back at his parents, as well as, other family members for their help in ruining his marriage to Deloris. Novadec knew one thing for sure that Deloris would never take him back. He tried many, many times before the divorce. Now with their third child expected in a few months, he plans to stay with Nora until the child was about a year old. In the meanwhile, he would get a house for her and the children. Since the farm was not doing well this year, it would give him an excuse to job hunt.

Novadec qualified for several positions offered to him. He was leaning toward a position with a company, which did business all over the country. This way he can justify being away. He had been saving his money because he saw this day coming a long time ago. He never let Nora know how much money he had. One thing messed him up was that last pregnancy. He had no intentions of having a third child with Nora. In fact, they were all mistakes because Nora lied to him. It seemed like he used her and trapped himself. He had to love the children because they looked so much like him. It is just that, they had the wrong mother.

Novadec could barely take his eyes off Deloris. He found every opportunity to hang around her, at the family reunion and, it did not go unnoticed, especially by Nora. By that evening, they got into a very heated argument. Deloris never encouraged any kind of relationship with Novadec, on her behalf. Any conversation she had with him was of a general nature; such as Sonja's schooling, their farm, her job and sometimes he asked about her plans. She talked to him about taking full responsibility for Sonja's financial needs. Novadec thanked her, but he wanted to do whatever he could for his daughter. Deloris said no more. Deloris stayed at the Family Reunion until everyone got there and the picture taking session was over.

Nora had retired to the house. Deloris wanted to say good-bye to her and made sure she knew that there was nothing between her and Novadec. When she walked in Nora was lying on the sofa, in the family room.

"Hi Nora, I missed you from outside." Not wanting to let on that she knew about the fight with Novadec. "I guess that little one inside wears you out, especially in this weather."

With a sly grin, Nora faced Deloris. "Yeah, you can say that again. How is your, job?" "It seems promising, but the one I wanted, I couldn't take because of Sonja."

"What's with Sonja?" "Novadec's visiting rights."

"Did you ask him about moving further away?"

"Yes, but he said he wanted to be able to see her as often as possible. Well, anyway, I don't want to rob her of his attention, because it's not her fault that we split up. I also want her to know her sister and brother. You don't mind do you?"

"Oh no."

"Good, because I want her to not only love my side of the family but her father's as well. One day I may remarry, and she may want to spend more time with her father. I was looking for you to join us when we talked this afternoon. What I had to say was for your ears as well as Novadec's. I expect he will talk to you about it."

"Why don't you explain it to me. I never seem to get any answers from him."

Deloris explained the most important part of the conversation she talked to him about. There was a lot more he talked about. Intimate things she always refused to respond to. He was always apologizing for what happened in their relationship, but she encourage nor respond. She merely brushed him off with a brief response.

"Well, that part of our life is over and done with. You have moved on, and so will I." Novadec would always question Sonja about Deloris' friends. To find out if any of them were men. He didn't realize how much he hurt Deloris. Novadec was her first and only love. She was a little afraid to trust anyone totally anymore. She had one guy who worked at the same company she did, and they would go out to lunch sometimes. He had been pressuring her to allow him to take her out some evenings. So far, she had not committed herself. When Deloris walked by anyone, women or men, they tend to turn their heads and take a second look. Deloris was not a pretty little chick, she was strikingly beautiful. She was about five feet eight and weighed about one hundred and fifty pounds. Her weight was well portioned throughout her body. Her hair was just pass her shoulders and she kept it in a pageboy style. It was kind of old fashion, but she was the only one around who could wear her hair that way and look good. She had dark, not too thick eyebrows and eyelashes about a quarter of an inch long, nut brown smooth skin, no blemishes and her nose, lips and ears just seem to just fall in line with everything that was beautiful about her. She was so casual about everything. She was just an everyday person. Sonja was beginning to look and act just like her. Deloris never overdressed. When she visited friends with children, most times you would find her on the floor playing with them or teaching them how-to-do games.

Deloris never sat down and held a conversation with Nora before. She found her pleasant and apologetic about a lot of things. Deloris got the impression that Nora was sorry she got involved with Novadec. It seems like all they ever do is argue from the day they got married. Nora believed she had to pressure him. Nora had been wondering, for some time, whether Novadec was the same way with Deloris.

Now that she had gotten Deloris to talk a little, she decided to ask. "Deloris, did you and Novy argue a lot when you two were together? If so, how did you handle it?"

Deloris was taken aback for a moment on that question. "Well, n o, not until about the last year of our marriage. Wait a minute, let me correct that. He argued, I didn't bother to listen because I always knew what I was going to do regardless of what he said."

"How can you not say anything when someone always calls you stupid?"

"Nobody ever called me stupid; if they did, I would laugh in their face because I know who I am and what I want out of life. It bothers me very little what others think of or about me."

"This family sure didn't have very many positive things to say about you." "I know."

"Then why did you come here today?"

"You know I normally drop my daughter off, but this time I decided to stay for a while. Each year they do invite me and I had wanted to talk to you and Novadec. I thought this would be a good time."

"Oh, do you plan to get married anytime soon?" "Soon...no.. but I hope to one day."

"Do you have someone in mind?" "Nope!"

"Are you seeing someone special?"

"I date one special guy," Deloris' smile came to almost a chuckle. "I date, let's leave it right there."

Both of them were laughing when Novadec walked in with Sonja by his side, "Well, what are you two up to?"

Sonja walked over and sat by her mother, indicating that she was ready to leave. Deloris was taking her to a show, which she was anxious to see. She put her arms around her mother's neck and kissed her cheek.

"Mommy can we leave now? We are going to be late. Mommy, can Daddy come with us, please mommy?"

"No Honey. You were with daddy almost the whole time we were here and now your other sister and brother want to have some time with him."

"But mommy they have him all the time."

"Honey, Daddy works almost all day every day and when he gets home he is tired, so he doesn't get to be with them a lot. Maybe, when Daddy has some free time, he will take you to a show you like. Now let's go before we are too late."

"But Mommy, you didn't wait for Daddy to say anything."

"Okay, I am sorry. I guess I was out of line." When Sonja turned to her father, Nora looked at him with fire in her eyes. Novadec didn't bother to look her way. He must have known Nora would have explored if he agreed to go with them. So he reintegrated what Deloris had said.

"I'm sorry Honey, your mother is right. I really can't come with you this time. I'll pick you up next week so we can go school shopping if it's alright with your mother. I'll call you later in the week to let you know for sure, okay? Now come here and give me a big hug and kiss."

# CHAPTER 4

N OVADEC TOOK A JOB WITH ONE OF THE LOCAL FIRMS A FEW WEEKS before Nora had her baby. He was out of town when the baby was born. Since everything seemed to be all right with Nora and the baby, he didn't come home for a couple weeks. The company he worked for was local, but it did a lot of out-sourcing. He had to travel a lot and many times for weeks he was away.

Once he got home, this time he start to put his plans in motion. He had Nora start house hunting. When she found the house she wanted, he purchased it, outright. Novadec had saved up over the years because they lived with his parents and their home was paid for. Living there, they had very few expenses such as, purchasing food from time to time even that was not a big thing because they grew much of the vegetables and fruit. Mrs. Felder and Nora canned and froze the fruits and vegetable they needed each year.

Novadec's job kept him away more and more and for longer periods of time. Nora knew he was getting farther away from her and their marriage was going down the tubes. She starts drinking more and more. She realized that she was beginning to experience the payback of what he did to Deloris. She knew Novadec was married to Deloris the first time she went out with him. Yet, she felt she could take him away and make him belong to her because the family was on her side. She for some time now, realize, he never truly belong to her.

Also, she knew now what Deloris went through. Nora kept having babies early in the marriage thinking this would keep him home. Now after the third child, he doesn't bother touching her at all. He sends money home to care for the family When he comes home he keep himself busy working on the farm, in his spare time. Most times he stays at his parents' home, giving Nora some lame brain excuse why. Novadec doesn't even bother arguing with Nora anymore. If she tries to start anything, he will walk out. She had gotten to the point where she drank too much and has been going out with another guy. Many times she would drop the children off at their grandmother's and may not pick them up until the following day. She would still help out on the farm when they needed her. Financially, she had very little to worry about. Anymore she appears to hate the sight of Deloris because she looked so nice all the time. She didn't want Sonja around her house. She never said it outright, but the action was there. Sonja picked up on it when Deloris took her over to wait for her father. Nora felt that Novadec gave Deloris too much support for Sonja and that he saw too much of her. While at Nora's, Sonja mention that her dad attended a play at her school. This was one of those weeks that Novadec had not been home for weeks, but he found time to visit Sonja's school. After that she would constantly question Sonja and when she didn't give her answers she wanted to hear, she told her, "Sonja, I think it would be a good idea to wait for your dad at your grandmother's house." She responded.

"Then I won't get to see my brothers and sister. Can they come over and wait with me?"

"We will see, now tell me again, are you sure your dad did not come over this week. Did your mom go out?"

"No."

"She didn't even go out with her boyfriend?" "No, she stayed home with me."

"Are you sure she didn't stay home and wait for your dad.?"

You better not lie to me, because if you do, you will never come over here again, you understand.?" Sonja was upset, she never had a reason to lie to Nora, nor her parents. She couldn't understand why Nora was so hostile to her. She loved her brothers and her little sister. Sonja could not understand why her father chose to be with Nora.

She was so harsh, sloppy and her language was so vulgar. Her mother was gentle, kind and quite soft spoken, she never cursed.

She found it hard to believe her father could choose Nora over her mother. Each time she asks him about it, he would say "I made a terrible mistake." She often wondered how could anyone make a mistake like that,

# CHAPTER 5

A YEAR AFTER NOVADEC TOOK THAT JOB HE RARELY CAME HOME.
Sonja was lucky to see him twice a year. She had reached the point
where she didn't worry about if or when, he may come by to see
her. He would write or call but, that was nothing like seeing and
touching.

Sonja was doing well in school and her voice was becoming more
professional. People had begun to stand up and listen, singling her
out from among others. She got the lead part in one of the major
productions during her sophomore year at the high school. Then
things begin to happen. After that performance, the instructor really
began to recognize her talent. Sonja had been writing a lot of her
songs and the music. She was allowed to sing one of her songs in the
musical. Her songs were mostly about the things she knew best, the
people she loved, what she wanted out of life and how she felt about
a problem situation or the likes. This one was about her and the love
she had for the father she rarely has been seen lately.

It's good to wonder why. Why people live or die
Die away from a life they love
Love of things and people around and above

It's sad to have to yearn
Yearn for someone who has sworn Sworn to never
leave you with doubt Doubt which makes you feel
put out It's good to wonder why

Why so much sadness makes you sigh
Sighing to keep from crying
Crying because you are yearning

My heart is full of pain
Pains that hurt through my brain Brains which
wonder about your love Love that use to hug me
like a glove

It's so sad to have to yearn for your touch
Touch of my father means so much
Much of his love we use to share together
Together, I wonder is it gone forever.

Deloris was always there for Sonja. That meant a lot, but it seems like it is always that other part of you which is not there worries you the most. Sonja was more of an introvert, but Deloris seemed to know what bothered her the most. Novadec was always so loving, and Sonja miss that. Sonja wanted to see her brothers and her sister, but Nora was impossible, so Deloris knew it was best she stayed away. Novadec called several times asking her to fly out with Sonja, but Deloris had a job and many times Sonja had classes. Both of them came to the conclusion that it was no excuse why he could not fly in himself. He prevented her from landing a much better job because she wanted Sonja to be where her father could see her often. Deloris kept Novadec abreast of the progress Sonja was making. She also made sure he was aware of performances; she was in, far in advance. He would send money to help Deloris with Sonja's expenses from time to time, although it was less frequent, the call came less as well. The visits were almost nonexistent. Sonja survived. It didn't take her long to realize that it was useless to want something you cannot have, life must go on. You can make it by doing things to fill the void and make things happen, or you can sit around moping and wait for things to come to you. Deloris kept

Sonja interested in making a life for herself and not worry about others or what they think. She must do things that are pleasing to and for her, but make sure she thinks things through before making decisions. She let her know that she will always be there to discuss her goals for life. Every so often Novadec's family would show up when Sonja was performing at the school or local theater sometimes they would bring Nora's children. It pleased Sonja greatly to see that the Felders practically kept them all the time.

Novadec and Nora got a divorce by the time their baby was two years old. Shortly thereafter Nora became almost incapable of caring for the children. She drank herself into a nervous breakdown.

Every so often, since Sonja became so popular, Mrs. Felder would call to ask Deloris to bring her out to visit her and the family. Deloris didn't break any records or dates to accom-ate them, but she would take her out from time to time to visit, at her convenience. After the way, they treated her she had long since gained their respect by not turning out like Nora. She, herself, was a very upstanding person in the community. She was quite active in the school system as a volunteer. She used a lot of her vacation time to help with school productions and to go away with Sonja's class on trips, also when Sonja had engagements on of town. Sonja received a scholarship to one of the most prestigious music schools in the states. Because of the distance, Deloris had to leave work early once a week to take her to the class.

It was quite an ordeal for Sonja to spend so much time on her studies. Especially when a couple of her schoolmates lived right in the neighborhood, a few doors from her They were quite active in sports and also boys. Many times "Can't you call and explain.?"

"No, they are always teasing me because I never come to any of the school activities." "Honey, come here and sit down, we must talk."

"What's there to talk about.?"

"Lots." Very grudgeously Sonja flops down, in the chair, at the table.

"Honey, there are no two people alike. Each has their own talent and interest, that is why the world is so exciting. If we all like the same things, there would be no challenge."

"Is that why you and dad broke up.?"

"No, I don't think so. Most things we shared the same likes and dislikes. There were very few things we didn't. There was one problem we had, though. He wanted me to help on the farm because that was what his family wanted. Because I loved him, I tried, but I hated it."

"He must have felt like you because he left and got another job."
"True, true, well Honey that's a whole different story.

Getting back to you young lady. I realize you have given up much of your time to voice lessons and singing at various places, singing at places your school mates rarely attend, if ever. If you feel like slowing down or quitting, I will understand. However, I would like to ask one favor, please go take your test tonight and give it your best. I would also hope that you would never give up completely because you are so talented. The academy selected you over two hundred other applicants for the scholarship, not because we could not pay for your lessons, but because you exemplify an observance amount of talent, which they felt they wanted j to help develop in their school. I want you to know, if you have real friends, they do stand by you regardless of where their interest and yours as well lie, even when it differs. They will not make fun of the choices you make. They will support you in every way.

*A friend is a great person to have indeed*
*But they cannot always respond to your needs*
*Friends have problems it's true*
*And they will not always be there for you.*

*We must constantly respect the absents of one another*
*And embrace the presence of others*

*Life is definitely not all it seems*
*If one feels that way, it can only be a dream.*

*Friends are a blessing up front*
*And in disguise*
*When they do not respond to your immediate need*
*Be a little wise*
*Don't throw your friendship to the weed.*

*Allow your love to be a growing concern*
*Never look back Reach up and out Have very little*
*doubt A friend is a friend*
*When you are a friend.*

"Okay Mom, we better hurry. Is the food ready?" Sonja did not give up her voice lessons. She did alter them a little to take some time to be involved with activities with her classmates. Some of her classmates still chided her about the choices she made to be so involved in and with the Opera, but she brushed them off without being rude. Yet, some of them attended some of her performances more than once and learned to respect her for her ability to do so well. She was treated with a range of specialty. Sonja had some sitcom experience on television which made her stand out as well.

In Sonja's junior year in high school, she fell in love with a schoolmate, from a distance. Timothy E Coil was a senior and one of the leading scorer on the Hockey team. He was quite popular with the girls. Sonja caught his eyes because she was not one of the droolers always in his face before and after games, nor hassling him in the halls and classrooms or pushing herself on him.

She was popular in her own way. More so with the elite. Tim was tired of easy girls pushing themselves on him. He wanted a challenge. So when Sonja starts coming to the games he noticed her right away because she was hanging out with some of the droolers but she was different, he could tell she was not one of them.

When they ran over to congratulate him, she stood on the sideline watching them. The following day after one of the games Tim met Sonja in the hall. She was on her way to class.

"Hi, there, did you enjoy the game last night?" "Hi, oh yes, and you were good."

"Thanks, last night was the first time I saw you at one of my games." "I came before with my mother."

"Oh, your mother likes hockey?" "Yes."

"What about your father?"

"I think he does too, but he doesn't live with us." "Oh, parents divorced?"

"Yes."

"How long?"

"Since I was three."

"That long huh."

Sonja reached her class. "I better get in, don't want to be late, see you."

"Why don't you stay after school and watch me practice and I will take you home afterward." "My mother is expecting me home right after classes."

Sonja disappeared in her class, left him standing alone. Normally girls do not do that to him, if anything, the class will start without them and he got the attention and they leave, when he let them go.

When Sonja got home, she told her mother about Tim. For the next couple of days, Tim looked for Sonja in the hall during class changes. She had gotten to the point of waiting for him to walk her to one class or another. She kept her mother posted on what was going on between them.

"Mom, I think Tim likes me and I like him. If he asks me to watch his practice today, I am going to stay. Will you pick me up about five thirty if I'm not at home today?"

"Sure Honey, Why don't you call me at work and let me know."

"Okay Mom, that's a better idea. I'll stay today because tomorrow I have to go for my lessons." Sure enough, Tim did ask her to stay and she told him she would.

Their school was noted for their hockey games because it was the largest arena in the area. Most all the local games were played there.

Tim had gone out with several girls in the school. It was rumored that he had gotten one of them pregnant, but no one really knew for sure, because she suddenly moved away. Sonja did not honestly know very much about Tim, only that he was a senior and a good athlete, highly respected by his teammates and teachers. It seemed like every girl in the school wanted to go out with him. She gave very little thought about him until he started giving her so much attention, even though she was only sixteen. She was falling in love with Tim. Sonja started attending most of his games and stayed to watch him practice when it did not interfere with her normal routine. Deloris allowed Tim to drive Sonja home after she gave Sonja some explicit instructions on the facts of life, touching on all details to make sure everything sunk in.

The last time she picked Sonja up from watching Tim practice Sonja got in the car very reluctantly. "Mom can I stay a little longer? Tim will bring me home."

"Honey, it seems like it was understood this morning that I would be picking you up, so why the sudden lapse of memory?"

"Mommy, I think I more than like Tim and I think he feels the same about me." "Oh, hum, are you trying to say you are in love with Tim?"

"Yes Mom, I guess so." "You guess?" "Mommy."

"Honey, I am not going to say it's not love you feel, but you are still quite young to be tied down to one guy who will be going away to college before too long and will be living among many girls his own age. You are sixteen. He is eighteen. How far do you think this relationship will go?"

25

"I don't know Mom, but that doesn't stop me from being in love with him."

"But Honey, how do you know if he feels as strong about you? Look, Baby, I don't want anyone to set you up for one purpose then walk away leaving you hurting inside. Okay Honey, I want you to know that I trust your judgment. Anytime Tim wants to bring you home after practice, it's okay with me, but you must promise me that you will not allow him to ruin your life by encouraging you to take any kind of illegal substance or force himself on you by other means. I am not saying he use drugs and drink alcohol. I am only saying if. Also, don't believe it when anyone say that the first time you have sex, you can't get pregnant that is a total myth, less than a minute will do it. I am saying these things to you because I love you and I want you to grow into adulthood and not be pushed. I am not going to talk to you about birth control because that is something should be discussed with your husband, when you marry."

"Thanks, Mom, I understand and I do remember all the things you told me and why." "Okay Baby, it's so hard to see that you have grown up so soon."

"Mom, then it will be okay if I accept a date if Tim ask?" "Whew, I suppose so."

Sonja was the envy of the female population at her school because of Tim. She went on her first date about a month after she was allowed to stay for Timothy E. Coil's practice. She was a bundle of nerves getting ready for her first date, even though, they were only going to an early movie and then to the Spring dance. Deloris was a bundle of nerves because her first impression of Tim was not good at all. On a scale of one to ten with one being the worst, Tim was about two and that was because she gave Sonja credit for giving him a thought by selecting him. However, she felt that regardless of what she thought or said to Sonja now, very little would set in because she feels that she is in love.

Sonja didn't give up or slow down on her singing, she even added more feeling to it. One thing Sonja learned in her young life was never to devote yourself totally to anyone person or thing. She knew she was in love with Tim and she also knew there was something her mother didn't like about Tim, but she wasn't saying anything. She decided to call her Dad.

"Hello, Dad."

"Hi Baby, I haven't heard from you in a while, Is something wrong?"

"No, and yes. Mommy and I are fine. What I want to talk to you about is my boyfriend." Right away, the first thing daunted in Novadec's mind is that his daughter was pregnant.

"What's with your boyfriend?"

"Well, Daddy, Mommy said it's alright to date him if it's what I want to do, but I don't think she likes him."

"Did she say why?"

"No Daddy, she will not say anything."

"Then why would she allow you to date him?" "Daddy, I am in love with him."

"I see, then even if she dislikes him that will not stop you from being in love with him? Is that what you are saying? Then I can understand why she hasn't said anything. So, Honey, I believe you have answered your question. Then as far as I can see it, it's best that she doesn't add to your frustration."

They teased her because she missed a school dance or game. After a while, it started getting to Sonja. She came in one day from class, Deloris was getting dinner ready hurriedly so they could make her class on time.

"Honey will you hurry with your homework so we can eat and get ahead of the traffic?"

"Mom, I don't want to go this evening. I want to go to the school game tonight. A couple guys in my class are playing their first game of the season."

"But Honey, it's important that you attend tonight. You have a test." "I know, but I still don't want to go. Can I take it the next time?"

"I believe tonight is most important. There will be other games.

Go tonight, then let's sort of plan the evening you want to miss because I took off work early in order to get you to class on time."

"But Mom, none of the other children my age are doing what I am." "That is because this is not where their interest and talent lies."

"I promised Tina and Martin I would go with them this evening. They are going to be waiting for me."

"Oh, Daddy, when are you coming home? I miss seeing you. I haven't seen you for almost two years. Don't you ever take a vacation?"

"Honey, I try to get you to fly out, but you are always so busy. I may be transferred back soon, but I don't know when or for sure. I guess Mommy is not home yet?"

"No Daddy and I hope you do come home soon."

"Is Mommy getting ready to get married anytime soon?"

"No, I don't think so. She hasn't said anything to me. Daddy are you still in love with Mommy?" "Why? Does it show?"

"Oh, Daddy." Sonja sort of changed the subject because she did realize she answered her own question. She was never disrespectful to her mother, but she knew if her mother and she had words or disagreement about Tim she may say something to her to prove her point. Sonja also liked to tease her dad about her mom because she knew that he had a lot of respect for her. She noticed the way he watches Deloris, whenever she talked to him, he would always ask a lot of intimate questions about Deloris.

Sonja had become shockingly beautiful like her mother and Deloris kept her dressed fashionably at all times. From the top of her head to her feet. Their home was kept immaculate by not forgetting to put things back in its place, yet it was well lived in.

From time to time they had a guest for dinner, some people Deloris worked with and the guy she went out with on occasion. His name is Fred, he worked with Deloris. Fred was nice and a real gentleman. He liked Sonja and was very proud of her. He was always there encouraging her whenever she performed.

Sometimes he even took her for her voice lessons when her

mother got stuck at work and couldn't get out on time. Fred was a good friend, but he could never replace her father, nor did he try. Sonja knew he had asked Deloris to marry him, more than once, but she would not commit herself. She would always say she would have to think about it a little longer. They got along well together. Fred went along with whatever decision Deloris made because he was very much in love with her and he didn't want to push her. They enjoyed each others company eminently.

Sonja's relationship had accelerated with Tim. They were seen together often. She tried to mix her love life with her singing. Each time they put on a performance, the school would allow her to sing one of the songs she wrote. It was usually done at the beginning because Tim's games and practices sometimes start right after the show begin. He did not make Sonja's performances often. In fact, he only made one of the performances out of three. Sonja was still happy about the way things were going in her life, but one thing still bothered her, her mom still felt the same way about Tim. She did her best to overlook any negative thoughts she believes her mother had about him. Sonja and Tim would go out about once a week, usually to a movie or if there was a school dance, to the beach or some culture museum. They really were too young to go any place else or at least Sonja was. Tim was far from the angel Sonja thought he was. He not only smoked cigarettes but other stuff as well. He had also picked up on alcohol as well because both his parents drink quite heavily. They were always having parties at their home or going out to one. The Coil's allowed their children to have drinks with them often. So it was only natural that they felt it okay to drink any time they choose as well as offer it to their friends. Tim had a habit of taking a drink as soon as he came home from school or practice, also before he went out.

A couple times when Tim kissed Sonja, she thought she detect alcohol on his breath. On one occasion, she asked Tim. "Have you been drinking?" He jerked his face away.

"Who me? Now Baby," Then he pulled her back in his arms.

Sonja just let it pass, not really thinking about it anymore Sonja was around Nora enough to know what all sorts of alcohol beverages smell like. However, where Tim was concerned she took it for granted, maybe he only taste a drink or maybe she was wrong. A couple times Tim offered her a drag off a cigarette. Then there were times she thought he was smoking a cigarette, but it didn't really look like a cigarette nor did it smell like a cigarette, yet when he came over to her it was a cigarette and smelled like one. Sonja only pushed all her suspicions aside and continued to love him. There were times when Tim held her too long, too close and too tight, she tried to overlook that. Sonja would discuss some of these problems with her mother. Deloris told her to be careful and it would be a good idea not to date so often. Deloris left early one morning for work because she had to fly out with a team of other engineers and would not return until late that night. Sonja had broken her date with Tim the previous week to fly out to help her dad pack. He would be moving back by her seventeenth birthday.

Novadec had shipped most of his things back and Sonja had been busy helping him to get them in order when she had any free time from school and practicing. Tim had called Sonja several times, but she was not at home and in school he missed her because he was tied up with sports and classes He would be graduating in a few month. They just kept missing each other. He was upset because Sonja was not at his last game. He wanted Sonja and didn't know what to think. No girl ever quit him before and no way was Sonja. Sonja had gotten tied up with helping her father, she did call his house and left messages, apparently his sister forgot to give him the message. Tim finally caught up with her in school.

"Hi Babe, what's with you? I can't seem to reach you anymore."

"Tim, hi I called your house and left messages. Didn't your sister tell you?" "Oh, she was mad at me for the last couple weeks. Can I see you tonight?"

"Okay, but I can't stay out long, my Mom is away and will be back late tonight. She wants me in by ten."

"Oh, okay, that's alright with me. I miss you. I'll be over as soon as I get done." He kissed her on the cheek.

Tim liked to pick Sonja up when they had free time to go out and eat (some fast food restaurant, because he couldn't afford much else) Tim's parents had a fairly decent income. They felt that it was not their responsibility to support their children's girl and boy friends. If they wanted to date, they had better earn the money to pay the expense. Tim had no time to hold down a job because of school and school hockey teams. He wanted to go to one of the best colleges and he needed scholarships. He didn't want to come out of college owing thousands and thousands of dollars before he finds a decent job. Suppose he wanted to get married and start a family, with a big debt over his head it would be difficult. Tim liked Tim, and Tim liked a good time. He liked the excitement like his parents have. Party, party almost every weekend and sometimes during the week. Rolling out of bed, half drunk and off to work. Because of the nature of their work, they sometimes get plastered at some of those luncheons they attended.

Tim and his brothers and sisters were raised in daycare centers until school age. When the first child was old enough to drive they invested in a good inexpensive used car and that child was responsible for transporting the younger one around, when necessary. Tim was the third of five. The oldest had finished college, got his place and moved away. The next was still in college. Tim and his other siblings were still in grade school. Because Tim had to be out so late with practice and games, always needing a ride home Mr. Coil bought him a car. It wasn't new. He got a good buy on it. The Coils like the recognition they received because of Tim. Tim knew, because of his activities, he could get over on his parents, like getting a couple extra dollars to take a girl out. His parents especially liked Sonja. She too was a positive new item and so pretty, as well as intelligent. They were constantly encouraging Tim to bring her over more often. They invited Deloris over to a dinner party, but she was tied up with some other function that

31

night and could not come. Deloris had heard about their parties and was glad she had an excuse because if not, she would have made one up. She felt that one day she would like to meet them more socially, but not right now. She had met the Coils briefly on two occasions. They sat with her at one of Sonja's performances

Sonja's school and the local community had an excellent program for youth who demonstrate the voice ability to become an opera singer. There have been a couple other opera singers who came from the same area. They now belong to some of the famous opera companies in the world. Sonja's instructor told Deloris that Sonja was the best she ever worked with and if she continues, it is no doubt that she will be among the others. One of the important things was that Sonja like to sing. When you like something, it makes learning easier. Since Sonja started seeing Tim, she did not practice as often but she was still holding her own. One other thing which helped Deloris was that the instructor had this slight falling away built into her program. When you are working with youth, as the instructor explained, you have to prepare for this," she said.

"Mrs. Felder, don't forget we know we are in the real world and your daughter is a beautiful young lady involved in a future career which demands a lot of her time.

At the time of her age, so few youth are traveling in her direction and others maybe teasing because of the choices she is making for herself. Whatever you do, do not force-just talk." Delores was relieved. She had invested a lot of time and money in her daughters' development, up to this point. She sure didn't want it to end right there. Tim came over that evening after hockey practice. Sonja hurried home because she wanted to surprise him with dinner.

He told her how much he enjoyed the dinner and afterward they listened to tapes. Tim tried to encourage a lot of hugging and kissing, but Sonja discouraged it. She spoke up, "Tim, I think it is time for you to leave now."

"Why, don't you like me kissing you anymore?"

"Let's say, no more tonight. I am not ready for marriage and children."

"Who said anything about marriage and children? There are such things as birth control, you know."

"Yes, I know." Still holding her in his arms.

"Do I have to leave? I could stay until your mother comes." "No, I think you better leave now."

Tim not wanting to upset her and wanting to leave on a good "note" hoping to be invited again when Deloris goes away like that, he said. "Okay baby, I'll see you in school tomorrow."

He never went with a girl this long without scoring. Many of Sonja's family came out to her performance. Also Deloris' Mom and Dad, and some others relatives from afar. Most of her mother's family live quite a distance away. Novadec was the proud father sitting beside Deloris with Fred on the other side. This was Tim's first time seeing Sonja perform.

When Sonja came out, she got a standing ovation. She sang this song for Tim.

*I want so much to be the women by your side*
*To hold your hand*
*To be there for you for every occasion*
*At night when you fall asleep*
*And the morning when your eyes open wide*
*Don't go away from too far*
*People like us must alway be together*
*To listen to each others heartbeat*
*To turn tears to smiles*
*And seal each other like a cap on a jar.*
*We have shared many wonderful moments*
*Of talks about our future*
*Of kisses and hugs*
*While we watch the sun go down*
*Unaware of any torment.*

*I want so very much to spend my life by your side*
*To be there for you always*
*And you for me*
*Don't ever play with a heart*
*Because it breaks easily*
*And then it cries.*

After the performance, a lot of the family came back to Delores house. She had anticipated that they would. So that day she prepared some extra Hors d' oeuvres just to be on the safe side. Sonja's seventeenth birthday was being celebrated that same evening. Delores had invited a few of her friends over, in addition, to the family. Sonja never cared for birthday parties. Only a few friends or out to dinner with her parents and maybe a few other relatives. Deloris found out just how much Sonja liked birthday parties when she was about twelve. Delores had noticed that had Sonja neverla lot of telephone calls and friends over, like the average twelve-year-old. So she decided to contact some of the families she knew in school, church, neighbors and the family to plan a surprise birthday party. She had her stay over Novadec overnight so she could get everything together. It was an outdoor party. Deloris had tables set up all around the yard.

In one area she music and a place to dance. All kind of food, buffet style and a bar-barbeque grill continuously rolling off hotdogs, hamburgers, chicken, ribs, corn-on-the-cob. Most young people would have jumped for joy. The decorations were outstanding. Deloris had a couple of her friend from her job help. They brought their children as well. The whole scene was like a Hawaiian Island. The cake was decorated with pineapples and coconuts. The icing on it looks like grass with a little umbrella all around it. Little grass skirts were at each place setting. The twelve candle sat in little pineapple candy in the center of the cake was the GOOD LUCK candle in a candy shape coconut. Deloris had invited twenty children Sonjas' age and about twenty relatives show up. It didn't bother her how many because she had had enough food and favors for everyone. Some relatives brought their little one. Everyone was there at the party before Sonja arrived.

When Sonja walked in everyone shouted" HAPPY BIRTHDAY" "SURPRISE" "SURPRISE" Then start singing the birthday song. Sonja gave her parents a half smile because she knew they meant well. Sonja never cared very much for phony people.

She knew how snotty many of her classmates were in school and in the neighborhood they tease her and make fun of her singing- even the ones at church. She knew they didn't really come to wish her a happy birthday. She also knew that her relatives on her father's side didn't know it, but she overheard them many times talking about her mother. Saying things like "she think she is better than everybody else bleeding Novy for money to spend on that kid saying she don't have to do this or that." Sonja knew her mother had talked to her dad and told him he didn't have to give her money for me because the farm wasn't doing well financially and that she would be alright without his help. It was her dad who wanted to do what he could.

What hurt her most was most of those comments came from her grandmother Felder and her aunts. Her Uncle Rivers was the only one who spoke up for her mother, but he was not always around. When Sonja saw all the people there, she thought ("Why did Mommy do this? I told her how most of those people are. She has been nice to all of them, but it doesn't help.

They only came to have something else to talk about. Why can't my daddy people be like my mommy people? They never say bad things about my Mommy or my Daddy. Whenever I talk to grandma, she always says, "How are your Grandma and Pop Felder and your daddy's brothers and sisters? Say hello to them for me."

I know my daddy likes my Grandma and Grandpa Whitman. They are like my mommy, they don't talk bad about anyone, nor do they hate anyone. Mommy never talks bad about any of them either. Not even Nora and daddy left us for her.

I guess mommy thinks this party will bring our family together and I will have more friends. Well, I will go blow out those candles and mingle a little while, but not for long.

Everyone was having a good time at the party. Almost time for the party to end Novadec wanted to dance with his daughter. He looked all over for her. He went to see if Deloris knew where she was. "Deloris where is Sonja?"

"I don't know, in fact, I haven't seen her for a while. I took it for granted she was over with the other children."

"No, that's the first place I looked."

"I better go look for her." She walked around a bit looking and asking a few people, but no one saw her. So she decided to go upstairs and look in her bedroom, maybe not feeling well or something. There she was sprawl out on her bed fast asleep. Deloris quietly set down beside her, leaned over and kiss her softly. As she stirred, Deloris whispered in her ear. "Howdy."

Sonja turned over facing her mother and smiled. "Hi, Mommy." "You okay?"

"Yes, (Lying a little) Just tired."

"Honey, Daddy is getting ready to leave and would like a dance with his daughter before he leaves. Then after everyone leaves we will talk."

"Okay, Mommy."

Deloris knew it was more than being "Being a little tired."

Sonja led the way out the room, down the stairs and outside where everyone was. She spent the balance of the time with her guests mingling. Novadec stayed for a short while to help put some things back in place.

After everyone was gone, Sonja went in and sat down to wait for her mothers' lecture. When her mother came in, she explained her reason for leaving. Deloris understood. Realizing her daughter was right in many respects. After that Sonja always approved any activities relating to her birthdays.

# CHAPTER 6

DELORIS JOB EXPANDED AND ON OCCASIONS SHE HAD TO TRAVEL A distance to help out. So far, she only had to spend the day away and was able to return home by late evenings. She didn't mind so much because Sonja was able and old enough to care for herself.

Sonja would always take Deloris to the airport early mornings so she could use the car to go whereever she had to. Deloris would always get a ride home from the airport with Fred, taxis or someone else. Whenever Novadec knew that Deloris was going away for the day, he would always stop by to see if Sonja got home alright. One particular evening Sonja made dinner for Tim. After practice, Tim went home to shower and change his clothing before going over Sonja's. The weather was bad and practice end early. It was kind of chilly out so he took a stiff drink before leaving. By the time he reached Sonja's house, he wasn't feeling any pain.

That drink on an empty stomach went to his head almost immediately.

He rang the doorbell and Sonja opened it as if she was waiting there for him. No sooner than when the door open he took Sonja in his arms.

"Hi baby, is my dinner ready.?" Smelling the alcohol Sonja backed away quickly. Rather coldly she spoke.

"Hi Tim, how many bars did you stop to?"

"Ah come on baby, it's cold and wet out. I needed something to warm me up until I get here for you to finish the job. Come here and kiss me." Pulling Sonja in his arms, kissing her over and over. Sonja tried to push him away.

"Tim, please let me go."

"No baby, I need some loving from you." "Tim please."

Tim began trying to undress her. She was steady fighting him. He picked her up and tried laying her on the couch. Sonja still struggled to keep Tim off her. She began to cry. Still fighting. Because of Tims' urge to get to Sonja, he failed to close the door behind him.

Just when he thought he was about to get the best of Sonja, Novadec walked in. He was so angry he picked Tim up with one hand and literally threw him out the door. Sonja fell into her fathers' arms crying out of control. Novadec set her down, cuddling her until she got a hold of herself.

"Alright, baby?" He question

"Yes Daddy, I am sorry."

"Sorry, sorry about what?" Taking a hold on her chin and bringing her face to face. He smiled. "Sorry, I made him stop?"

"Daddy, thanks, I am so very glad you came by." "I am glad I came by as well."

"Now young lady, what was he doing here?" "Daddy sometimes I cook dinner for him." "Does your mother know about this?"

"No, not really."

"What does no not really mean? Does she or doesn't she?"

"Daddy I thought it was alright. I did it before and he never acted like that. I think he was drinking alcohol."

"Oh, have you ever had drinks with him?" "No Daddy, never."

"Did he know that Deloris was going to be away late?"

"Yes, that is why I invited him over to keep me company for a little while."

"Baby, don't you ever invite a guy over when you are alone in the house, not knowing when your mother will return because you are asking for trouble."

"Okay, Daddy, I am sorry. Now I think I know why Mommy didn't care for Tim very much. Daddy, I have never experienced such behavior from him before. I was in love with him and I thought he understood."

Novadec went on the explain many things about life from a man's point of view. Sonja interrupts several times with questions.

"Daddy do you feel that way about Mommy before you got married?" "Uh huh, but because I loved her so much, I respected her wishes."

"Then, I suppose Tim never really loved me as much. I don't think I will ever speak to him again, Dad."

"If you do, make sure he understands how you feel about his actions tonight. Baby, I have been smelling something good, every since I came in. Did you two eat up everything.?"

"No Dad, I haven eaten yet."

"I haven't had dinner yet, how about fixing something for me."

"Sure dad, we never had a chance to eat." "Good, come on, feed me, young lady."

Novadec stayed until Deloris came home which was about one a.m. When Deloris saw Novadec's car in the driveway, she knew something was wrong. Sonja was in bed asleep so He explained what happened. Deloris cried out. "I knew it, I knew it would happen sooner or later I had a bad feeling about him. I never liked the way he undresses my daughter with his eyes. He seemed like he was waiting for the most opportune time. Novadec, I knew it. Is she alright? He didn't do anything to her did he? I would kill him if he did anything by force to my baby. That creep."

"Deloris, she is alright, nothing happen." "Oh, thank God."

"I hope she understands why I had so little to say about their relationship."

"I think she does Deloris and I think you should have told her why you felt the way you did about Tim."

"At age seventeen, Sonja is still sweet and innocent. She took a person for their word. She wants to believe that all people are good, kind and in different when you treat them with love and understanding and you believe they love you."

"I suppose you are right."

39

"However, I believe, this incident with Tim will help her to grow and be more cautious." "Yes, and thanks for coming by. Heaven only knows if she had to fight her way out of that situation."

Sonja fell into a troubled sleep that night. She was sure she loved Tim and thought he loved her, but now, she didn't know.

Tim was embarrassed and at the same time angry. He just knew Sonja would blast his name all over the school about the incident. Tim tried to contact Sonja that hold weekend to apologize. She knew he was drinking and just maybe he could use that as an excuse and she would understand, even if her parent didn't. Anyway, why did she invite him over when she was alone and at night while her mother was out of town?

What did she expect? She knew he wanted to go to bed with her. No one could be that dismal. All the girls he knew he thought were going the distance. Tim murmured to himself

"She is so gorgeous. She must have gone out with other guys before him. She must know the ropes and how to protect herself from becoming pregnant."

At their school, there was a high teen pregnant rate. Parents who help cover up the mistakes a child made will send them away until the child is born and when they return, they claim adoption or another relative. Then there are the ones that are out of school for a week or so with minor surgery (abortions).

Sonja had perfect attendance so that claim cannot be placed on her. So she had to know how to take care of business. Tim was sick with worry so he decided not to go to school that Monday. If his name is out there, someone will call him.

Sonja went to school as if nothing happened. She didn't mention the incident to anyone. Her only hope was that Tim was not injured when her father threw him out the door. When Sonja did not see Tim in school, she thought he was hurt when her father threw him out. She did want to see him so she could really tell him what she thought of him for pulling that stunt on her, drunk or not. She knew he knew what he was doing.

Tim called Sonja just about time the time he thought she got home from school and before her mother got in from work. He was praying she was home alone.

The telephone rang no sooner than Sonja put her books down. Thinking it was her mother checking to see if she got in alright.

"Hello, Mo ..." "Sonja."

"Oh hi Tim, did you want to know if I was alone so you can try that stunt again?"

"Sonja no. I want to say I am sorry. I suppose I had too much to drink and it went to my head. Please forgive me, it will never happen again."

"I am quite sure of that."

"Are you saying you will not go out with me again?" "Exactly."

"I guess your parents will not allow you to huh?" "No, it's not my parents decision, it's mine."

"I suppose I am not the right guy to make love to you? If not, then who were the others?"

"Just what are you trying to say? That I sleep around with anybody? I hate to disappoint you, except that I don't. I have no intentions with you nor did I with anyone else, for your information. Also just to set the records straight, I invited you over because I loved and trusted you and thought you understood that. Now, I am sorry you misunderstood me. I don't think our relationship can ever go any further."

"I didn't want to hear you say that." Tim was afraid to ask Sonja did she tell anyone about what happen.

He knew he had to face up to whatever. So he returned to school the following day. Tim attempted to talk to Sonja at school. She responded to the conversation in a very general sense.

After a couple days at school, everyone began to notice the cold shoulder Sonja was giving Tim. They start asking questions but, neither Tim nor Sonja revealed the reason for the breakup.

*Love can be like a morning glory It opens early*
*spreading wide Spewing out its wondrous fragrant*
*From all sides.*
*After a while the old buds fall*
*Then another grow anew*
*The vines continue to grow*
*With more flowers of purplest blue*
*Young love is quite fragile*
*It travels along the morning glory vine*
*Blooming and falling off, blooming and falling off*
*Soon they come stabilized on a plastic line*
*We shall all reach that moment in time*
*It is good- can be fine*
*But would be great if we could forever bloom*
*On the morning glory vine*
*That early rush into forever love String along the young*
*and sweet A vine which breaks many times*
*Will cause a continuous pursuit with an open mind.*

Sonja bounced back without a lot of heartaches because life had taught her that things you seem to want the most change. Many times, they change for the better but, you cannot see it right away. She remembered when her mother and father would pick her up from the sitter and sometime grandma Felder, it made her so happy, she ran from one to the other kissing and hugging them.

Then things changed. She was with her mother and did not see her father for days. It was hard to understand. Many times she overheard her father talking to her mother in anger.

That too was hard to understand. She was glad to some degree that her father was not around to hurt her mother's feelings. She still loved them both and it was easier to do so with them being separated.

The evening she saw her father emerge from the bedroom he and her mother slept in many times, and then Nora came out afterward.

She was confused. Her mother took her hand, in tears, immediately turning around, leaving Grandma Felder's house where they planned to spend the weekend with her father.

She knew something was drastically wrong. Sonja returned full time to her singing lessons and trying out for various parts in the opera companies close by. Between school and singing lessons, she had little time for anything else.

She got many parts in the opera companies because she had such a special quality in her singing because she put so much of her feelings into her songs. Deloris and Novadec hired an agent for Sonja, someone who could be trusted to travel with her sometimes. Neither of them could do it because they had to work to help pay for her expenses. Novadec had to take custody of his other three children.

His mother helped him out a great deal. Then sometimes she would not lift a finger to help because she still rejected Deloris and because, of that, they felt Novadec was spending too much money on Sonja. Actually, Deloris was paying almost all Sonja's expenses. Novadec had purchased a house and the mortgage payments were pretty high for him alone with three children to support.

He was unable to work any overtime because of the children. Many times when Sonja was performing close by he would take the children to see and hear their sister sing. In fact, they would spend the night over Deloris's, just to be with Sonja many times. When they stayed over, Deloris would take them with her because they were proud of their sister. Sonja loved them as well. She was over her father's and many times she would bring them home with her. Novadec loved every moment of it. He was around so much he had almost pushed Fred out of Deloris's life. Because of Sonja, it had gotten so that Deloris found herself helping with the children more than enough. Nora had remarried and moved away. Before she moved, she sold the house and kept all the money.

She kept the children for a short while, but they were being so mistreated by Nora and her new husband. Mrs. Felder kept them of an on. Then that stopped. The children gave them a hard time when they had to go back to Nora. They never wanted to stay with their mother.

Nora got a good price for the house because Novadec made sure it was kept up properly for the children's sake. He tried to get a part of the money to help him, but she refused. One thing Novadec was sorry he did not stipulate that the house be in trust for the children, instead of just putting Nora's name on everything. However, at the time, he just wanted out of the marriage but, also provide for the children. Tim still tried to talk to Sonja, but she had very little to say to him. She never went to the games any longer.

All the girls were after Tim, but Tim only wanted Sonja. He never had a girl so tender and loving, but yet, stood up for and by certain moral principles. She trusted him and he let her down. He felt bad because he went by Deloris's job one day to apologize for his behavior. When he caught up with her, she was on lunch. He walked over and sat down before she could say anything. "Mrs. Felder, please hear me out. I know you don't think much of me because of what I tried to do. I am here to ask you to please forgive me."

"Well, young man. I must say you are right about the way I feel. You know my daughter loved you very much and she thought you cared as much for her."

"Yes, Mrs. Felder. She told me and I feel very bad about what I did to destroy our relationship. I suppose I put her in the same class as some other girls I know."

"Look Tim, there are lots of decent young ladies out there who will not lay around regardless of how much in love they are."

"How well do I know it."

"Tell me son, when you get married do you want a women who is untouched or one that has been sleeping around with other guys?"

"Now that you mention it, whenever I think of marriage, I always think about a wife being with me for the first time."

"Then you were not thinking of my daughter as being your wife, in the future. You were only seeing her as being another little tramp."

"Oh no, I never thought of her that way. No, Mrs. Felder I never once thought of her that way."

When Tim left, he really had to search his soul. He had to wonder what was on his mind which made him try something like that. Forcing himself on Sonja. He thought it must have been the alcohol. From that moment on he never took another drink. After her conversation with Tim, Deloris felt a lot better about Tim. She even liked him a little. She knew it took guts for him to come to her. She found out later he also went to Novadec and apologized. Tim invited Sonja to his graduation, but she did not go. Tim worked all summer. He also attended a lot of Sonja's performances. That Fall he went away to college on a scholarship. He was about five hundred miles away, but he still kept track of what Sonja was doing. Since Tim no longer drank he rarely dated unless it was with a group. During his first semester, his parents drove all the way the college to let him know he had gotten a summons to appear I court for child support. The child was by a previous friend name Wilma. She wasn't a girlfriend. They just hung out and she was in the group. She was very popular in school and left suddenly. She later said she had gotten pregnant by Tim, but he never knew, because she didn't tell him. When she got pregnant, her parents sent her to live with an Aunt out of the area. They were hoping she would choose to abort the child.

When Wilma heard that Tim was going out with another girl, she decided to have the child and make him marry her or pay child support. Right after that incident happened with Sonja, Wilma called and told him she had his child and what was he going to do about it? Time was a bit shocked and wondered why she had not let know sooner. Not that he would marry her but, he would work something out to help with the child's expense. He told his parents he might be the father, but he couldn't be sure. They said that if he was they would help until he finished college and get a job. But, he would have to repay them. He agreed but heard nothing until he got the summons. They handed him the summons in anger.

45

"I want to know why this came to the house. You were supposed to take care of this in a simpler manner. My children going to court. What other embarrassment you children are going to cause us?"

"Mom, I am sorry, but Wilma never got back to me and I tried to find out where she was but, they would not tell me. So after she didn't get back to me, I just thought she found out It wasn't mine."

"Well, then we will get a lawyer to look into it. Maybe you will not have to come home. By the way, you never told us what happen between you and Sonja. That young lady is going places. I hope you didn't mess around and get her pregnant."

"No. No mother, she is not that kind of girl."

"Thank God, anyway, I didn't think she was. That's the kind of girl you guys need to have and there wouldn't be so many children without fathers. Come on tell me, what happened between you two?"

"Oh mother, we are still friends."

"Yes, sure, you didn't try to force yourself on her and she quit you." "Mother, please. Dad talks to your wife."

"Well son, you are finding out about women. It's very little I can do because she is very inquisitive. In fact, I would like you to answer that question myself."

"Oh come on dad, give me a break. Do I have to tell you everything.?"

# CHAPTER 7

TIM'S PARENTS GOT A LAWYER TO REPRESENT HIM IN COURT AND HE didn't have to leave college that day. Tim questioned the fathering of the child within himself. There was something about that night he wasn't sure of. He was sure he was not alone with Wilma, but he was drinking, like the rest of them.

Tim was into sports quite a bit. Between that and his other studies and a job, he had very little time for much else. Less not forget, trying to keep up with what Sonja was doing. He wanted to see the child and hated to ask his parents for money. They were paying the support demanded by the courts, for the child.

Tim worked every weekend and some evenings when he didn't have a game or practice too late.

If he has a game on the weekend, he would go in afterward because the place stayed open late. Sometimes he was pretty sore but he still went into work. He worked as a waiter in a very exclusive restaurant, which was always busy.

It was a very busy, high level, ivy league type area. The people didn't mind paying the price for their dinner and they tip well. Sometimes Tim's tips for one night would be more than his weekly paycheck.

Tim wrote Wilma often to ask about the baby. He would send extra money from time to time. He was also saving money to go out and visit the baby when he had some free time. Wilma was living about seven hundred miles away. He got the chance to visit when the child was about four months old. That day he took the earliest flight and got there about nine in the morning. The trip took about two and a half hours because he had to change flights midways. The baby was a doll and Tim fell in love with him. Wilma named him after her father, whose name was Wayne. When Tim drove up in a taxi, Wilma was getting him ready for a nap. Wilma's aunt met him at the door. She had never met Tim, but she seemed to know him right away.

"Hi Tim, come on in. I am Wilma's Aunt Laura."

"Good morning Mama, I am glad to meet you and thank you. Is Wilma home?" "Yes, have a seat. Can I get you something to eat?"

"No thank you, I did eat earlier. Thanks for asking." She called out to Wilma.

She walked in with the baby. "Hi, Tim. (in a very snotty way) meet your son Wayne Richardson."

"May I hold him?"

"Of course. Would you like to take him home with you? Maybe your girlfriend will watch him for you.?"

Taking the baby and cuddling him in his arms Tom ignored the comments.

"Gosh, he is a doll. I wish I could take him with me, but I am in school. As soon as I finish school and get a job, I will take you up on that. If it's still on."

"Huh, I would like to go away to college myself but, who do you think I can leave him with twenty-four hours a day?"

"I thought your aunt was caring for him and you were in college."

"I am, but I said, go away to college. When are you getting married?" "Married? I don't even have a girlfriend."

"I thought you were going out with that little opera singer. What happen, you got her pregnant too?"

"No. No, not her. By the way, why didn't you tell me you were expecting my child? The call I got sort of told me you were not sure. Was there someone else?" "If I told you right away what good would it have done?"

"Well, I don't know but maybe I could have done a lot more to help you during the pregnancy." "Would you have married me?"

"At this point, I don't know. It's possible. You left without saying a word. Called me and said you may be having my child and I heard nothing else. I thought just maybe you made a mistake, decided not to have it or it belong to someone else. How was I to know anything when you never called back? I tried to find out where you were, but no one would tell me. What was I to think?"

"Well, I still want to know if you would have married me if you knew?"

"Wilma I .just got finish telling you, I don't know, but it would have been possible. What more can I say?"

"What happened to your little girlfriend?" "What little girlfriend?"

"You know, the opera singer?"

"Oh, you're talking about Sonja Felder. We just pal around for a while. Nothing much happened between us. We went out a few times."

"Yeah, sure, a few times. It seems like you could not wait until I left, from what I heard."

"Look, Wilma, I didn't come all this way to argue. We were never that tight anyway. We never dated alone. Even that night we were with a group."

"Why did you bother coming?"

Tim was getting a little fed up with the sarcastic way Wilma was needling him. Her tone of voice outraged him. She was always a hot head--wanting everything her way. She wanted Tim, but so did a lot of other girls and he knew it.

He was the star hockey player, good looking, as well as, in the top of his class. Wilma was a good student and popular but dumb in many other areas; like not protecting herself. She was angry with the world because she failed to control one aspect of herself (allowing herself to become pregnant). Now she wanted to direct all her anger toward Tim even though, he wasn't the only guy she went out with. Tim had reached a point when he was about to explore. He calmly handed Wilma, the baby as he said. "I think you better lie him down he is asleep. I'll stop back later."

"Where are you going?" "I said I will be back."

Tim walked out and never looked back. He didn't know anything about the area, but one thing he knew, he had better get out of that house. He could no longer stand Wilma's mouth. He also knew he could never even consider marrying her. Tim thought about Sonja, and how lovely she was. She was never loud or demanding. Even when he tried to take her, she never screamed, she cried and pushed him away. He wanted her so bad but thinking back, he didn't think, with all his strength she would never have given in. She was strong and determine. He knew she loved him then. He believes she still loved him, at least, a little. He could still remember the song she wrote right after they broke up.

> *I feel so sad about so many things*
> *I wished nothing could have ever gone wrong*
> *I loved you and life, for so many reasons Now the only*
> *thing left is for me to sing. Sing about the good times*
> *we shared*
> *Write the words which make the whole happy*
> *Keep my smile warm as the sun*
> *Keep myself happy and free from fear. Fear only make*
> *you want to cry Thinking of the love you want in life*
> *Never forgetting that life is for real*
> *And a lot about it makes you wonder why. Why life*
> *has to be this way*
> *Causing so many aches and pain Broken hearts,*
> *disappointment alike When the main ones you trust*
> *Never truly cared*
>
> *They only wanted to pick your brain.*

Tim had walked about ten blocks before he realized how far he had gone. He found a place to get some lunch. He ate, looked around a bit and started back to Wilma's Aunts house. He had another three hours before his flight left to take him back to the college so he took his time.

When he did get back, Wilma was still brooding and stewing in her stinky attitude. She tried her best to whip up and argument, but Tim would not follow her up. He just outright told her.

"Look, Wilma, I am sorry about what happened, but you should have told me. Don't expect people to read your mind. I didn't come this distance to argue. If that is what you think, I will leave now."

"Oh, then you just want to see if the baby looks like you, I suppose? Well, you can get a blood test if you want more proof."

"No, no Wilma, I'll take your word for it. I will not subject this little fellow to unnecessary test." "Then you believe he is yours?"

"Wilma, if you recall, I did agree to support him. I can't do much right now until I get a real job. Right now I only work weekends and some evening when I don't have practice to late. I am trying to send a little extra as often as possible. I wanted very much to see the baby and it took a while to save for the trip. I will be here as often as I can. When the semester ends for the summer and I can get a sitter I will take him, if it's okay. Please call if anything I can do, otherwise, I'll do my best." Shrugging his shoulders, as if discussed with his life, he tried to defend himself. Not really looking at Wilma but through her, he continued to speak. "I will continue to write because some days I don't have the price of a phone call. Please bare with me, you will not be sorry."

"Yeah, sure, bare with you, after you have ruined my life." "Hey, look, baby, I didn't do this alone."

"How well do I know."

Wilma's aunt came in and sit down. They talked for a while until it was time for Tim to leave. Tim expected the visit to be more cordial, but Wilma had a lot of built in hate for him. She didn't seem to be very tender with the baby either. Tim wished it was some way he could have taken the child. Had his parents been more settled, he would have asked, but they did more partying than he did.

After he had got back, he had an urge to call Sonja. He wanted to tell her about the baby. Sonja was getting ready for bed when he called.

"Hi, Sonja."

"Oh, hi Tim. How is school?"

"Great, a lot of hard work. Well, in fact, if you keep up with your work, it's not that bad. Not much different than high school."

"Oh."

"How is your singing career coming along?" "Great."

"Sonja, it's nice to hear your voice. Can we be friends?" "Sure, I suppose."

"Do you mind if I call you like this sometimes?" "It's okay."

"You sure your boyfriend wouldn't mind?" "Sure."

"Who is he?" "Don't have one." "Oh, good."

Sonja just lets that slide by without asking why it is good she didn't have a boyfriend.

Tim told her about the baby, Wilma and what happened on the trip out to see them. He told her how free girls had been with him and that it seemed like the natural thing to do. That was the reason he was so adamant about his advance with her. He really thought she wanted to be with him.

Tim explains that a lot of girls put up a fight, but it didn't really mean anything. It was just their way of trying to show they were not so easy, in-a-sense.

From the way other girls talked about boys and the things they did, Sonja understood, to some degree, why Tim tried what he did to her. They end their conversation when she agree to write him. Deloris came in when Sonja was about to hang up the phone

"Hi, baby, who was on the telephone?" "That was Tim."

"Timothy called?" "Yes."

"What did he want? Isn't he in college?"

"Yes, he just wanted to talk. He was upset. You know the girl he went out with before, had a baby and she never really told him."

"Never really told him, I don't understand,"

Sonja explained the details as the way Tim told her.

"Yes, I can buy that. Girls can be that way if they are not sure. You know Honey, after talking to Timothy, I kind of like him and I really believe he is sincere.You know what he told me?" Sonja raised her eyebrows, as if to say, keep talking.

You know what "He said, he believed if he had torn all your clothes off he still wouldn't have gotten anyplace with you."

"He is right because I was in the right position to ruin him for life. Mom, I was crying because I didn't want to do that. I only wanted him to know when I say no, I meant it. I was so glad when Daddy walked in. I believe he knows that Daddy saved his masculinity. Mom, now he wants to be friends and for me to write him. Do you think it's okay? I don't want him to think I fit into the category he has been judging girls by."

"Do you still like him a lot, Honey?"

"Somewhat Mom. I use to like him a lot until you know what happen." "Do you envision being his girlfriend again?"

"That's the farthest thing from my mind right now. But if you think it's okay to write to him, I will. Remember, if anything happens, I am going to blame it on you. Now, what do you say?"

Sonja was smiling as she made that statement. "Okay baby, since I don't want to be blamed for anything I'm not going to tell you to write to him."

"Oh Mom,.You are no help."

Teasingly Deloris said. "Go to bed, child." Reaching into the desk draw.

"Honey, here is some writing paper, envelopes, and stamps. When you finish the letter you can put it right there with the others, I'll mail it on my way to work."

Sonja smiled. "I'm going to tell my Daddy on you. Good night Mommy. I love you teaser mmmm mmmm."

Tim remained one of the star players of the team at the college and he continued on to excel academically as well as hold onto his part time job.

He continued to save his money and send Wilma a small portion. He would call Wilma at least once a week to see how the baby was. Most times she wasn't there. He spoke to her aunt. The aunt just outright told him that she was not properly caring for the baby and was rarely home.

She told him once when he called. "Timothy you seem like a caring person and quite concerned about the child or I should say the baby. Don't forget I know how they kept this from you and I also know you could have questioned his fatherhood, but you did not want to subject the child to any unnecessary pain."

"Mrs. Laura, I don't like to see little ones suffer for the stupidity of their parents. I know that I am not sure, but I will always love and care for the child because someone has to."

"Well son, I sure wish you could take this child because I am not pleased nor feel sometimes, that it is safe to leave him alone with Wilma. Believe me, she knows how I feel."

"At this point, I don't know what to do. Is it possible for you to take full charge of his care and I can try to pay you. Give me a figure of what you will charge. I can withdraw my payments from Wilma and transfer them to you."

"Look, son, I practically care for him almost totally now. Also, Wilma is my brother's child and there is not much I can do. I am constantly in contact with them. We will hopefully work something out. They are paying me to let her stay here because she had the baby out of wedlock. They do not want it known that their precious daughter had a child out of wedlock. For them, it is very embarrassing. Wilma's parents will be out in a few weeks. Then I will let you know exactly what they decide because something has to be done soon."

"Thank you, Mrs. Laura, I certain appreciate what you are doing for little Wayne."

"Oh thank you, it's my pleasure. I love children. I guess it's because I never could have any. My husband, God, bless his soul. I tried very hard and spent many dollars trying to find out why I couldn't get pregnant, but toward the end, the doctors found out it wasn't me. My husband is dead you know."

"Yes, I sort of gather that."

Tim was glad when the hockey season was over then he could work full time. His employer liked him and so did the customers.

He got another part time job assisting in a summer program for youth. His full-time job as a waiter was mostly late afternoons and nights. He was busiest on weekends. Tim banked every dollar he could, all except the occasional call to Sonja and Aunt Laura to hear about the baby. He also went out to see the baby again. Just seeing him again he felt that he had not made a mistake excepting the responsibility for little Wayne. He was growing up so fast. He had a lot of Wilma's features but looking more like her father.

Anymore, Wilma was never there when he called nor did he bother telling her when he was coming out to visit. His visits were there in the morning and back to his place that evening. This was because of his jobs. Tim was lucky he didn't have to pay for housing because of the summer youth program he was working with was sponsored partly by the college. When Tim was about ten, his teachers in school commented on several occasions about his voice. They felt it should be developed further. So his parents sent him for lessons. He was in a number of school shows. But by the time he was in junior high school he told his parents, he needed a break. It seems as if all the boys his age were into sports. As time past, he never went back to voice lessons. He never forgets what he learned.

He sang many times when he was alone, in the shower or in a group. Tim's reputation followed him all the way through school. He stood out physically, socially, academically and with such an appealing voice, was not easily forgotten. Teachers who knew him, when in a pinch would single him out to lead the National Anthem or sing it alone. He could compete with any baritonist just breaking into and opera.

Ever since he and Sonja quit whenever he thought of her, he'd find himself bellowing out one of her songs. He especially like the words in the song Sonja wrote and sang at the last performance he attended during the holiday.

> *It's a special time of year*
> *When the giving of yourselves is so sincere*
> *You can put away all your hate*
> *And turn on the charm*
> *Never pushing anyone away*
> *Just holding them close, in your arms*
> *It will make you wonder why anyone fight*
> *Because it's so easy to do what's right If you love me,*
> *don't wait to tell me During the holiday season*
> *Never hold back for that reason*
> *I need to know you love me always Because I want it*
> *to be for all the days Lover makes mistake and hurts*
> *each other Let's not do that anymore to one another*
> *We are all grown up*
> *Now it's time to change our views Because life should*
> *mean a whole Lot to me and you.*

Thinking back, Tim wondered if those words were meant for him. No doubt about it, Tim knew he was desperately in love with Sonja. He knew he had to finish college. He didn't have the money to go home as often as he liked because he had to check on little Wayne. That trip always took a big chunk out of his savings. Sonja wrote from time to time.

In her letters, she wrote about school, her parents, who she believes was getting back together, her siblings and performances she was in. She never wrote about their relationship. He would write about the little Wayne and how much he wanted to get married when he finish college and get a job Tim wanted Sonja to say she wanted to get married as well. He wanted her to say she wanted children. He wanted her to talk about them being together and she wanted to be with him. Tim hadn't seen Sonja for almost a year. He knew he had to see her.

He wanted to hold her in his arms like he use to and kiss her. If he could just be near her, he would be happy. Tim was so pleased when Sonja wrote and told him she would be singing at the opera house near his college in a month. She was replacing someone who was in an auto accident She would be flying out a few days before the performance for dress rehearsal and to familiarize herself with the cast and theater.

Tim had gone there several times when he was free. He had a couple small parts in a few productions. They paid him well as a stand in. He never told anyone about it on campus. He only sang a couple lines in the performance. Tim seldom took his singing seriously. It was only per se to him. Tim rarely hung out with the guys on campus because of his job and a lot of what they were into. There was always a party going on some place. He was invited but rarely show.

One party he had to attend was when the team got together and threw a surprise for the coaches birthday. He had a daughter about Tim's age. They had some classes together. Colleen, the coaches daughter, was the person who mentions to Tim about her father's birthday. She was wondering what to get him for his birthday. Tim thought it a good idea to discuss it with the team. They were all for it. Colleen helps with the plans. She liked Tim a lot anyway. This was a good way to get to know him better. Coach Ron Clark invited Tim over to his home several times with the encouragement of his daughter, but he was always busy. studying or working. Coach Ron liked Tim a lot because he was always respectful and did his part in helping the team to be number one. Tim was not a showoff nor pushy in any way. He earned his scholarship and repay by doing a good job. He never skips practice for any unnecessary reason.

Sonja had to come alone. Deloris had to work and her agent had a death in her family. She followed instructions quite well. Deloris trusted Sonja to fly out alone and someone will pick her up at the airport. She would be able to meet her the following day and fly back home with her.

Novadec couldn't make it either because of his other children. It would have cost too much for all of them and he couldn't take off from work that much time to drive out. Sonja has gone away alone before] so it wasn't a big thing for her. She was getting ready to graduate high school and would be going away to college that fall.

Tim found out what hotel Sonja would be staying in when he called her. Sonja had barely finished unpacking when he knocked on the door. Seeing Tim's face through the peephole made her remember what she thought she had forgotten. However, she had forgiven him but held herself in reserve. Sonja knew she still liked him but wasn't sure how to receive him. She opens the door.

"Hi Tim, how are you?"

"I'm fine." Staring at her, up and down. "My. my. you certainly have grown up." Not being able to resist any longer, he took her in his arms. "Gosh, I miss you, I have got to kiss you to make sure you are real." Sonja looked into his eyes and smiled making sure he didn't kiss her lips.

"Oh Tim, all those beautiful girls on campus I don't know why you would want to kiss me."

"None of those girls could measure up to you, in my life. I miss you, Sonja." "Tim please."

"Sonja I miss you so much." Tim took Sonja's arms and put them around his neck. Sonja pushed him away. He tried kissing her over and over, but she stood her ground, although she wanted to kiss him back. He never gave up.

"Baby I love you. Will you marry me? Please say yes. I need to know you belong to me." Sonja didn't know how to respond One thing she knew was that she was not ready to get married. She had to think fast because she was weakening.

She let her arms drop. Stepping back she looked at him. "Timothy Coil, do you know what you just asked me.?'

"Of course, and I meant every word I said. Now will yo----"

Sonja cut him off. "Tim I don't know what to say. You know both of us are quite young and really just starting out. I believe getting married is important and sacred. Planning ahead should go into it. Tim, it's not something to jump into. How will we support ourselves?"

"I can get a job." "What about college?"

"I can still work part-time like I'm doing right now." "But I will be starting college this fall."

"You can come here and we can continue to live at home. I'm sure that wouldn't be a problem." "Suppose I become pregnant.?"

"Are you referring to Little Wayne?"

"Not particularly, but he would be a part of our family. I am talking about me becoming pregnant."

"So, that is a part of marriage." "Tim, you are not listening."

"Yes I am and I know what you are trying to say. I suppose I am being selfish. Okay. Okay, but one thing I want you to promise me, is that you will marry me one day when we have a better handle on our lives."

"Tim, please don't ask me to make such a promise. I will say this, though, I do hope to be a wife one day and it maybe you. I am not sure."

"Okay, I will accept that and no matter where you are, I will remind you often. If you try to marry anyone else you better not announce it because I will most definitely do all I can to prevent it." Tim couldn't have his way nor could he make Sonja fall all over him, so he calm down and settle for a more meaningful conversation.

"Tim what are you going to do about Little Wayne? Will your parents take him until you finish college?"

"If we were married, would you take care of him?"

"Of course, he looks so sweet, I don't see how Wilma can mistreat him. Tim why don't you asked your mom and dad.?"

"I sort of hinted at it but, my parents never react."

"I know your sister will help with him. Tim, please ask." "Okay, if you insist. I will call them tonight."

Sonja wanting to get out the hotel room, away from being alone with Tim. She didn't want any questionable conditions to encourage a more intimate relation with him. She had feelings too.

"Tim I am going to go down and get a bit to eat. Are you hungry?" "Why can't we have something sent up?"

"Now. Now, Timothy let's not act risky. Come on, let's go over to McDonald's and see Roy Roger's, pick up a few burgers at the King or go to Kentucky for chicken fries." "Funny, funny, come on I know what you are driving at and I can't blame you." "Tim, I---I."

"It's okay Sonja, I still love you." A few tears start to trickle down Sonja's cheeks. Tim wiped them away, wrapped her in his arms, attempting to kiss her.

"Baby, I think we better go get something to eat, at least, get out of here because it is getting warm in here."

Sonja gave him a warm half smile and sort of pry herself out of his arms. Then they left. Tim skipped a couple classes to spend some time with Sonja.

She met him on campus after his most important class was over. Sonja's mom rented her a car, so she was able to pick him up and they drove around for a short while and she dropped him off at work. She went to her rehearsal and when it was over, shewent to Tim's .job and hung around until his shift was over. There was a lot for her to see and do, but time did not allow it. Tim introduced her to several people and when they found out who she was and why she was there, it was hard for her to get away from the questions. Many of the people there were expected to be there for the show. At least, that was what they told her.

When Deloris came to pick Sonja up. Sonja told her about Tim. She felt that Tim had finally grown up. Now able to restrain himself. He had also became quite responsible based on the things Sonja told her and about little Wayne. Deloris felt love for him. She too could not understand Wilma, her parents or Tim's parents. It was nice that they paid the fifty dollars a week the court requested for support however with the money they earned, they would never miss it. They spent much more than that on booze for their friends. Deloris felt that they should have taken the child. She knew they could have done better for the child. Both set of parents for that matter.

Deloris was helping Novadec out with the children quite a bit. They love to visit at her house and stay over. One of the children told Novadec on many occasions and they all agree.

"Daddy why don't you and Deloris get married so she can be our mommy? We want a mommy like our oldest sister, Sonja."

Novadec responded by saying. "Look, Baby, I don't have the final say where that's concern." "Well Dad, did you ask her?"

"No, not really." "Not really?"

"What I mean is, she knows how I feel about her. Just maybe she doesn't want to remarry me."

"But Daddy she did one time. Tell her the same thing you told her before and I know she will marry you. She likes us. Please, Daddy, our real mother doesn't care about us she rarely calls or visits. Do you want us to ask her? You do love her, don't you?"

"Yes, very much, but let's not rush things, because when I ask her I want to make sure she says yes."

"Okay Dad, but you better hurry because Fred keeps calling her. Daddy, I was just thinking." "Yes, what about.?"

"Well, the most frightening thing could happen." "What on earth are you talking about?"

"Deloris might agree to marry Fred before you even ask." Karla threw up her arms, walked out and went to her room. Novadec could only shake his head. Yes, he was very much in love with Deloris and a bit disturbed that Fred was still in Deloris's life. He thought he had crowded him out some time ago. He wondered did Fred ever ask Deloris to marry him and if he did what did she say. Novadec was sure Deloris knew how he felt about her. The farm was picking up again. He was doing his share of the work. With the extra money from that he could get his bills caught up and have some extra to take Deloris out to some places. She had helped him a lot, especially with the shopping for the children. Prior to that, he was spending a fortune. He did not know how to match things up properly for the girls. He wasn't much better with the Darwin either.

Through Sonja and the other children, he had gotten Deloris to do many things for him, even food shop and prepare meals yet, she kept her distance from him. Once he almost had her in his arms but, she dropped something and took her time picking it up. It appears as if she anticipated what he had in mind. Each time he tried to get close to her she found a way to ward him off. Novadec was afraid to damage the relationship they had by forcing himself on her. He wasn't sure of how she would react.

His parents were angry with him because he spent so much time around Deloris. He would ask Deloris to do things for him and the children before coming to them. When the children were around them, it was Deloris this, Deloris that Deloris said don't do it that way, Deloris, Deloris. At that point, they found out everything about who was doing what. When his parents question him about Deloris being around the children and why he did not ask their assistance, he said very little.

Novadec realized that he fell into their trap before and ruin his marriage to Deloris and he will never allow that to happen again.

Nora was a different story. She was pushed on him by his parents and he excepted what his parents wanted for him. He never loved Nora. The very day he married her, he realized that. He knew it was Deloris he really loved. Each time he was with Nora, he was pretending she was Deloris. He rarely slept with her. Most times was when he had a couple too many drinks. Nora was a product of what can happen to a person when they allow themselves to be molded by someone for spite. Novadec realized that Deloris would never have slept with him in his parents home before they were married. She would have thought it disrespectful. When they stayed at his parents those weekends while they were married, she kept to her side in bed. However, at home she slept in his arms every night. He lived with that memory night after night. Sometimes with tears, wondering how he could have been so dumb. He turned his back on his wife and allowed his parents to persuade him to accept someone like Nora to replace her. He wondered if Fred ever touched her. It made him insanely jealous just thinking about Fred being her.

Tim hated to see Sonja leave. He also knew that Deloris was beginning to like him. This made easier because he was head over heels in love with Sonja. Both of them understood and excepted little Wayne. Deloris asked a lot of questions about him.

She was amazed to find out he excepted fatherhood responsibilities without a whole of medical fanfare. Even knowing he was not the only man in Wilma's life, and that they shared only one close encounter. He told Deloris; "I felt since Wilma went to that extreme to blame me and the time she took, I didn't think it necessary to question her. The baby needs a father and I will do my best, but I could never marry her."

"Why Tim?"

"Deloris, I knew that, before we shared any type of relationship. She is a bit too wild and free with herself for me. Besides, that night we were both drinking heavily."

Looking over at Sonja as he continues to speak.

"Even then, if I ask, she could have said no. I almost ruined the relationship with the only person I ever really love and respect. I believe she loves me but when I try, she said no regardless of how demanding I tried to be. Because of it, I love her even more." Looking away from Sonja and back to Deloris continuing to speak.

"I don't know how I'm going to survive without her being nearby for the next year and a half. Sonja wants a career and as the man of the house I anticipate on being, I need a career, to earn the type of income to support my family. I know it would be selfish to ask her to give up any goals she may have because hers are just as important as mine. At least, that is what I'm trying to tell myself."

Everyone laughed. Deloris focused her attention on Tim.

"Timothy, you are quite a young man and I believe it will be a pleasure to have you as a son-in-law. Sonja told me you asked her to marry you."

After their discussion, Tim and Sonja went for a drive. He had her back in time to finish packing and get to the airport on time.

# CHAPTER 8

THE FIRST TIME TIM WENT HOME SINCE ENTERING COLLEGE WAS for Sonja's graduation. Because of his job he could only stay two days. Most of that time was spent with Sonja, which upset his parents.

They felt he should be spending more time with them because they were the ones helping him by paying child support for his child. Tim was somewhat upset with them because they never made a conservative effort to visit Little Wayne, especially when they were so close by.

He believesd they saw him once are maybe twice. Even Wilma's parents did not visit often. They only went when they had other matters of concern. Mostly problems Wilma's aunt had with her. Tim got all the feedback from Wilma's aunt. She made sure he knew what went on with the child.

Tim managed to get the same .job back that summer at the college as well as keeping his regular waiter job. Sonja started college right after she graduated. It was a special program she got involved in. She attends classes three days a week, living in a dormitory with a bunch of others girls. Then they all would go home for the rest of the week. This lasted all summer. The credits they earn help them to complete their degree in three years instead of four. She had time for her performances as well. During the Fall, she entered college full time. Her and Tim kept in contact, mostly by mail. They had little time for each other. Tim job, sports and studies and also Sonja studies singing and performances when she could make herself available. Tim would write and let Sonja know when he was going to call.

After the first semester, Sonja got an apartment with two other girls. With some of the money, she earned from the performances Deloris allowed her to use some to get a telephone. Deloris would only allow Sonja to use ten percent of the money she earned from the performance. The rest went into an account with Sonja's name only and her name as a just in case of an emergency. Deloris and Novadec, but mainly Deloris continued to provide for Sonja's basic needs. When she went to college during the summer, she had to have a car to go and come each week. It was too costly to stay in a hotel for four days or fly back and forth each week. Even though, she paid for the car, Deloris did not allow her to take it that Fall on campus.

When Sonja got the telephone both of the girl provided their portion equally without any problems. Each was responsible for their long distance calls and if they receive any collect calls. Sonja was fortunate to get in with a couples girls who were thriving for specific goals. They along with her had their heads on straight. Neither got on the other nerves with bad habits, such as drinking, smoking, hanging out or sneaking guys in. They all had boyfriends in colleges elsewhere and they were true to them. Their moral standards were high. Sonja would call Deloris once a week, just to keep her abreast of what she was doing. Many times she callsed and her father was there, which made her happy. Tim would call every other week. Most times he would reverse the charges and send her a check from time to time, more than covering the cost of the calls.

After Tim completed his third year of college. The college adminstration sports program was charged with trying to spirit a couple of students to transfer to their college. They were offered gifts to play for their college. So they say. The college denied it, but it didn't help what they said the college teams was suspended from participation in any games for a year.

It didn't upset Tim because he wasn't going out or trying for any professional teams. That wasn't what he wanted to do as a career. Now Tim didn't have to worry about those many hours and days of practices and games. Because of this he has more time on his hand.

When he wasn't working, he could visit the baby, Sonja or go home. He could also pick up more classes and get out of college early. Another thing, because of the suspension the summer job would be canceled. It was a good thing, though because Wilma's aunt called to say she had to go to the hospital as soon as possible for surgery. Wilma had not been home for a couple days, nor did she call. The school semester was just about to end. They had daycare on campus so Tim made connection anticipating bringing little Wayne back for a while. He flew out the same day. Aunt Laura was quite ill. The neighbor had taken Little Wayne. Aunt Laura was glad Tim got there when he did.

"I am so glad you are here. I have been praying."

Tim smilesd down at this wiry middleaged women. She never had children, that's why she loved Little Wayne so much, in spite of his rude mother.

"I am sorry it took so long to get here. As soon as you get settled in the hospital and I know you are alright, I will take Little Wayne with me for now, will that be alright.?"

"Of course, who's going to complain.?" Tim gathered what he thought the baby would need with the help of Aunt Laura they got a taxis and he took her to the hospital. The staff assured him that she would be well cared for and what will happen when she leave the hospital. He left that same evening.

None of the guys complained about Little Wayne, in fact, they helped Tim a great deal. He was a good, happy-go-lucky child. After the semester end, which was only a couple days Tim took him home to his house. Even Tim's parents fell in love with him.

When Sonja came home, the three of them were always seen together.

Tim called Wilma's aunt often to make sure she was doing well. He was hoping his parents would keep Little Wayne because he had to return to work. He managed to get a few weeks off. Two weeks they were closed for some renovations. He likes the job because it paid well. A full week work he could clear about three hundred dollars, not including tips.

During the semester when he worked part time, he cleared about two hundred dollars after taxes, not including tips. His tips, most times were two to three times that much.

Aunt Laura called to let him know Wilma was coming to pick up Little Wayne. She didn't really want him. She was doing it for spite because her sister told her she had seen Him and Sonja together with Little Wayne a couple times. Tim thought it only right that he bring the baby over to visit with Wilma's parents and Sonja merely tag along and why not? Wilma's Parents didn't like the idea of having Little Wayne around Sonja. In fact, it seems as if they were jealous of the way Sonja cuddled him in such a loving manner. They could tell she loved him very much and they knew their daughter Wilma hated the child and only kept him for spite. If it was any way she could inconvenience Tim in any way she would, but since he along with Sonja showed so much love for him she would take him away as long as she had Aunt Laura to take care of him.

# CHAPTER 9

As soon as Aunt Laura got out of the hospital and was on her way to recuperating, Wilma came home. She was dropped off by some of her friends. She was a little concerned when she saw her aunt lounging, which she never did. Always up and fully clothed, and no Little Wayne or his toys laying around.

"Hi Aunt Laura, where is the brat?" "Where have you been?"

"Oh, didn't I tell you I was going skiing with my friends?"

"No, you did not. When does a mother take off for this length of time, leave her child, without saying a word to anyone, least of all, to the person who is suppose to be helping her with the child?"

"I am sorry Aunt Laura, I thought I told you. Now where is the little brat." "He is with his father."

"Just what are trying to tell me."

"He is with his father. I was quite ill, didn't know where you were and somebody had to take care of him."

Wilma was so angry, she was interrupted by the telephone before reaching a point of indignation. The phone was right beside Aunt Laura, so she answered it. "Hello--yes--I am fine, thanks. Yes, here she is. She just returned. Wilma, it's your sister." Wilma gave her aunt a half smile and teasingly snatched the phone out of her hand.

Wilma's sister gave her a blow-by-blow description of what she observed between Tim, Sonja and Little Wayne. Her sister meant no harm, she knew how Wilma felt about the child, but what she said was anything but favorable with Wilma. She didn't like the idea that the two of them appear to be playing the part of loving parents and Little Wayne seems so happy. Wilma's sister was not trying to make her jealous. She only wanted to let her know her child was doing fine and not grieving over their separation. Little did her sister Galina realize the thoughts her sister Wilma had concerning Tim. Nor did she realize that she care soooo very, very little for the child. However, she knew how selfish she was and how the child seemed to be a burden to her. But to hate.

Galina was glad when Wilma was sent away. She was far from as pretty as Wilma. Wilma never lets her forget. Yet, she always tried to be as loving and caring for all her sibling Yet, many times it was hard not to scratch Wilma's eyes out Wilma took the first flight out the next day to pick up Little Wayne. Galina picked her up at the airport. Wilma had her go directly to Tim's house where they found Tim, his brother Benjamin and Little Wayne playing ball. When Little Wayne saw Wilma, he dropped the ball and ran to Tim, burying his head in Tim's chest. He appeared as if not to want to see Wilma's face. Not bothering to speak to either one, Wilma reached for Little Wayne, turning him around facing her.

"Hi, baby, come give Mommy a hug." Still hugging Tim, he mumbled. No, No." Wilma trying to insist by pulling him.

"Come on Baby, give Mommy a hug, come on." "No, No." She looked over at Tim as she spoke.

"You can get his things together, I taking him back the first thing in the morning." "What's the rush? Are you working or something."

"How is your Aunt feeling?" "She's okay."

"You're sure? because I could keep him a while longer and bring him back when you say." "That's okay, I'll take him now."

"Wilma, can we talk about Little Wayne for a few minutes?" "What's there to talk about?"

"I would like to keep Little Wayne when I finish school and get a job, for sure, however, if you want I can take him now for good."

"Are you planning on getting married now, right now?"

"No. At the college, they have a nursery and daycare. Also, my roommates don't mind helping with him. In fact, they were a big help when I took him there when your Aunt went in the hospital."

69

"How many women do you room with? Does your little opera singer live with you as well?" Tim knew he had to play Sonja down in order to make Wilma realize, it was he who wanted Little Wayne and Sonja had nothing to do with it. "Who are you talking about? I room with two guys. I can take care of the baby and I have a lot of time to be with him. Come on, what do you say? I know it will not be that easy for me, but I want to have a go at it."

"What's the matter, you don't want to give that little fifty dollars a week, to help support him?"

"No, no, that's not it. I wish I could give a couple hundred, just to prove to you I want to help care for him. I know that is a very small amount of care for a child, but it's the best I can do until I can do better. I do send extra when I can. Now, what do you say? You will not have to worry about him at all. I will take full charge. You can pick up your life and move on and see him anytime you want wherever we are." Tim didn't know where he would begin if she said yes, but he was willing to take the chance. He felt that a lot of women lived on campus with a child and or attend college with children, so, what's wrong with a man doing the same. He envisioned his parents helping in some way! He hoped. If it were necessary to drop out for a while, he would do so. He hoped Sonja would marry him a lot sooner. Wilma's aunt shouldn't have to be bothered with such a small child. She is still under the doctor's care. From what he had heard, he strongly believe he could get the child through the court system, but he didn't want to involve her aunt extensively because of the things she would have to admit. Although, she seems to be ready and willing, but he didn't want to ruin any family relationship. If she told the courts the things, she told him it would infuriate her brother's family image in the community. Tim knew Aunt Laura was fed up with Wilma and felt sorry for the child. However, because of her, Little Wayne receives the best of care by her. Little Wayne was the child she never had and wish she did. Wilma was unsure of Tim's motives behind taking Little Wayne so she decided against it by saying.

"I have to think about it. I'm not sure I want to give him up completely." "I told you-you can see him whenever you choose." "Maybe your wife would not like that."

"I can't answer that because I do not plan to marry anytime soon." "You mean, your little opera singer will wait on you forever?"

"Wilma, if you are referring to Sonja, she has her career to think about right now, not a husband and child."

"From what I heard, she look like she would be willing to give all of that up for you and my child."

"Well, my dear, I think your hearing is all wrong." very snotty, Wilma interrupted. "Well, anyway, I have to think about it."

Tim was getting angry because of her attitude and fired back, trying to control himself. "I don't know what you have to think about. From what I understand, you are never around to take care of him anyway. It seems like, whenever I call, Aunt Laura never knows where or when you will be returning. I would like to know what kind of game you are playing with Little Wayne." Just then Sonja drove up.

Hi everybody." Little Wayne tore away from Tim, making sure he didn't get near Wilma. He ran into Sonja's arms.

This irritated Wilma. Galina and Ben stopped their conversation to watch him. He almost knocked Sonja down getting into her arms. Wilma walked over and snatch him out of Sonja's arms. Little Wayne began to scream, fighting his way out of Wilma's arms. This irritated her even more.

What prevented Wilma from showing her true relationship with Little Wayne was when Galina went over and took him. Everyone there could tell he wanted no part of his mother. Wilma was so embarrassed. She led the way to the car.

"Come on Galina, bring him along. (Barely turning) I'll be back later to pick up his things." Tim was upset. "What about our conversation?"

"I told you I'll think about it." Wilma left.

Everyone felt so helpless. They hated to see Little Wayne leave feeling so sad. Looking back, reaching out with sad eyes as if saying "Please don't let them take me away."

For those few days, Sonja grew very close to Little Wayne. She seems to feel a special hurt when Wilma took him out of her arms. He fought and cried hard for her. Tim put his arms around her as they walked in the house. Ben said nothing. He knew Tim was hurt.

Tim looked down at Sonja. "Honey, she only took him for spite. She doesn't give a hoot about that child. If her Aunt Laura weren't taking care of him, she would have him sitting on my doorstep or long since put him in an orphan. I asked her to let me keep him. She said she will think about it. Tomorrow I am going to my lawyer to see what other steps I can take to get him."

"I am glad, Tim because I could feel the hurt and fear in that little boy the moment he touches me. I know he is still looking and watching for us to come and get him."

"I wish we could, Baby, I wish we could."

Fortunate for Little Wayne, Galina took care of him and she decided to return with them and spend some time with her Aunt Laura. She told Tim when she came back for Wayne's things.

Tim was pleased and Sonja and Ben relieved. Sonja still felt the little body against hers. She thought to herself. 'He is so little, too little to have so much fear of his mother.'

*One day when all my dreams come true You won't*
*have to cry anymore Because I'll be right there for you*
*As I watch you go away, all I could do was cry*
*If I had the proper control*
*You would be right here by my side*
*I hated to see your sad little eyes*
*Begging for me to rescue your little heart*
*But after the tears I could only sigh The trepidation is*
*extremely hard Because life can be so, cruel*

*Trouble flashes and destroys like a lightening rod*
*Your eyes were asking, why don't you save me*
*How could I make you understand*

*There was nothing in my power to set you free From*
*a distance, I could feel your heart Pondering a- with*
*hopelessne-s and fear*
*Confused by the separation, knowing we will be apart*
*You were saying, what did I do wrong*
*Please take me out of these arms*
*I'm so little and weak, help me be strong*
*One day when my dreams come true*
*You won't have to cry anymore or be strong*
*Because I will be your strength.*

Sonja had to leave for college that summer because she was in that special program every summer where she attend class three days and home four. She was also still active in the opera company and performing quite a bit. She was beginning to get offers for some leading parts in some of the best opera companies. One was for Susanna in the Marriage of Figaro. She sang the lead in AIDA. She did extremely well in AIDA and received some positive critic acclaims for that part.

Tim attended many of her performances because he had more time, but when the Fall semester started, he took and abundance of credits, as much as the college would allow. He still held onto his waiter job.

Tim managed to have the same roommates all doing the time at the college. They got along swell, but they could not understand Tim, he never went out and was always studying or working. When there was a day or two they had no classes, if he had the money, he would go check on Little Wayne or rent a car and took that long trip to visit Sonja. However, that didn't often happen because she was almost five hundred miles away.

Wilma still would not make up her mind about him taking control of Little Wayne. Tim didn't push the issue because it would have been very hard for him especially with the hours he was working and the extra classes he was taking. He knew he was well cared for by Aunt Laura. If he were in the total care of Wilma, he would seek custody legally the day she came to pick him up at his parent's home.

Deloris kept Novadec's three children while he went away for three days on a business trip for his job. He had to represent his company at a conference. He tried to get out of it but, the person scheduled became ill and hospitalized and there was no one else capable of doing the presentation.

The children were supposed to stay with their grandparents, but they beg to stay with Deloris. When they found out that their father was going away, they called Deloris without Novadec permission. When they asked, she said, "Okay."

The children were never a problem and besides, she missed Sonja. Novadec was happy because he will have a reason to spend more time with Deloris. Maybe a dinner out to show how much he appreciated what she did. He will get the chance- to call her and check on the kids or use any old excuse to call and talk to her. He was so much love with her. He kept trying to wait for the right moment. Because he was so ashamed of what he done, it seemss like that moment never comes. When Novadec returned from his trip, he went directly to Deloris's house to pick the children up, they had just finished dinner.

"Hi, Daddy," Darwin spoke first. "You had a nice trip?" "Yep. Were you kids on your best behavior?"

"Yes, Daddy."

"Okay, I get your things." "Do we have to leave now.?"

"Yes now." They all finished putting things away and hustled up to get their things. Novadec walked over to Deloris turning her to face him.

"I want to thank you." Deloris looked into his eyes and backed away.

"Oh, no thanks necessary, it was my pleasure." It seemed like lightening struck Novadec. He took hold of her arms.

"Deloris, I am sure you know that I am very much in love with you and I want more than anything for you to be my wife again. Please say you will marry me, please Baby. I can't take this loneliness any longer." He pullsed Deloris in his arms and kissed her over and over. What brought them back to reality was the children's call from upstairs. On his way out his last words were. "I will be back as soon as I get the kids settle over their grandparents. He was back in less than an hour. Deloris had just emptied the dishwasher and was putting the dishes away. When he rang the doorbell. He picked her up and sat her on the couch. They talked for about two hours. He had to get back? Pick the children up and get them to bed. They had school the next day. He did not leave until she agrees to so he would find out everything that had to be done and, if need be, pick up all the paperwork, notify Sonja and a few other friends and family members. That night Novadec called Sonja, she was elated. She was the first to know. As soon as the exact date was set she would be coming home. Deloris tried to get him to wait a month but wouldn't hear of it. If they could have got married, the next day would not have been too soon for Novadec. She gave him a time frame and allow him to make all the plans. The children were overjoyed. His family was happy for him because his siblings knew how hurt he was about the breakup. He leveled his grief on them many times. They knew how their parents were because they tried all kinds of tricks on them, but they put their foot down and made them stay out of their business] whereas Novadec fell right into their trap.

Novadec and Deloris would not be taking a honeymoon right away, maybe sometime in the future. When they discussed it, he merely states unequivocally, that the most important thing is that they will be together. They will have some time alone when the children to be with their mother for two weeks if he can pry them away.

Tim was still carrying an over abundant of college credits, trying to finish before four years. Wilma's had got -ton seriously ill again and had to be hospitalized. Tim contacted Wilma to try and get her to let him have Litte Wayne. By now his parents had gotten so concerned they agree to take care of him until Tim finish college. Tim was attempting to go through the legal system, but they were so slow. He was overly concerned because Aunt Laura was in the hospital. Where Wilma lived, right around the corner was an apartment complex. Many, many people with cars would scoot around the corner without worrying about who was in the street. Nobody complaint because most of the people who had children, had nice yards in the back of their homes and on a rare occasion you see children in the front of their homes.

Wilma was holding Little Wayne hand, on her way to the bus stop when she stopped to talk to a neighbor who was asking about how her Aunt Laura was. Little Wayne got tired of just standing. He started pulling on Wilma's hand saying, "Go, go." He continued to pull on Wilma's hand. Finally, let go of his hand, still talking and not noticing, Little Wayne wandered, in the street, right in front of an oncoming car. It's probable that the driver did not see him because of the curve he was coming around. The car knocked him in the air and his little body landed in front of a car coming from the opposite direction. He died instantly. All Wilma could do was stare. Once in her life she didn't know what to do.

The lady she was talking to fainted. A neighbor who met Tim several times called 911 and then proceeded to call the college where Tim was. She had his number because he had gotten some information for her. Tim had it so anyone could leave him a message and normally he try to check it everyday. It so happens he was in the area tutoring. So when he got done, he when over to check his messages. He was stun. For a few moments, he didn't know what to do. Tried to call Wilma and no one answered. then he called Sonja and left a message. then he calls his mother at work. She could tell something was wrong when she heard the first word.

"Mom"

"Hello Timothy, what is wrong."

"Mom I don't know what to do. A neighbor of Wilma's just called and said Little Wayne got killed."

"What.?"

"Mom, please see what you can find out for *me*. She said he just got hit by two cars."

"Okay son, I 'll make some calls. You wait right there. I'll get right back to you." She called Wilma's parents. Wilma just calls them. They were making arrangements to go out right away. They assured Mrs. Coil, Tim's parents they would call her as soon as they find out the details. Mrs. Coil called Tim and told him to stay put until he hears from her.

He argued the point, but he knew she was right.

The Richardson was somewhat perturbed with Tim for trying to take full custody of Little Wayne. They did not like anyone to consider their family members as inept or incapable of doing anything. Tim waited around because he knew Sonja would be calling him. She had given him an outline of her activities and she stuck be them. Sonja called about twenty minutes after his mother. He explains what happen. Sonja was upset because she had fallen in love with the little guy. She was also anticipating on being his mother when she and Tim marry. In fact, she was looking forward to it.

Tim flew out the day of the funeral. It was just a few family members. Tim's' parentsl his sister and brother, Mr. and Mrs. Richardson, Galina and a few of Wilma's friends, as well as, Aunt Laura's neighbors. Aunt Laura was still in the hospital. Tim did not know that no one told Aunt Laura. He decided to go to the hospital for a visit before leaving to thank her for all she did for Wayne. When he walked into the room, she smiled.

"Why are you so dress up?" That's when he realized Aunt did not know. Since she was so kind to him he felt that she should know, regardless of what the family says.

"How are you feeling?"

"I am doing good. Every day a little better. How is my baby?"
"That is why I am here. He got hit by a car."

"He is dead, isn't he?" "Yes, I'm sorry to say."

"I knew it and I bet my niece is responsible. You don't have to say it because I know she is. Timothy, I am sorry."

"Aunt Laura, I tried so hard to get custody."

"I know son, and I know my kin folks. I wonder what they think of their precious daughter now?"

"Well, I have a plane to catch. My parents had to get back but they say the next time they are out this way, they will stop by and visit."

"And you better visit me too. I will never forget you."

"You know I will and I will never forget you, Aunt Laura."

Sonja wanted to come to the funeral, but they thought it best she didn't. The casket was closed anyway because the little body was crushed.

Tim returned to school and buried himself in his school work and on the job. He and Sonja talked often. He began more than ever to save money. He wanted desperately to get married.

One of the largest opera houses in the area were staging performance. It is to benefit the oompany. They normally do this every two years. The tickets are very costly and are sold out no sooner than they are put on the market. This performance usually serves another purpose which is to select some growing participants to sing a major part in one of the leading operas.

Sonja's advisor at college gave out entry forms to all of the classical music and voice student to apply for a part in the show. Sonja, along with a couple other students got together and made plans to go for tryouts She didn't tell Tim she would be nearby because she wanted to surprise him. The tryouts were to be held on a Saturday night. Sonja and the others students arrived that Friday the part she was trying out for. She took the bus to Tim's place.

Tim's roommates had gone home for the weekend because their classes were done until the following Monday. Sonja taps on the door. A familiar voice said, "Come in. the door is open." When Tim saw Sonja, he jumped up, picked her up and threw her on the bed. Caressing her in his arms and kissing her over and over. He reached a point where he was ready for any and everything. He whispered

"Baby. you are going to spend the night with me?" "Tim no, You know I can't do that."

"Why?"

"Because I can't."

"You can if you want too. I need you, Baby. Right now. Please say yes. Please, Baby."

"Tim." Sonja got up from the bed. Tim was angry. He reached for her. She continues to say no. Tim was getting angrier.

Sonja reached a point when realized it was time to leave. Tim made one last plea.

"Baby please." "Tim,"

"Don't Tim me, you know I want you. If you don't love me then why did you come here. There is the door. Go." Through many tears, Sonja ran out the door. She manages to get a bus back to the hotel a few minutes after she reach the corner.

She was glad no one in the room she shared with the two other girls. She cried a bit longer and then took a shower She waited for the others to return so they could go to dinner. She was quiet the rest of the evening. No one really notices because they were excited about the show. Sonja got in the mood with the others, she figured, she would deal with her problem with Tim later. Right now she had to get her mind on her reason for being there.

When Tim came to his senses, he couldn't believe what he did. He wanted to scream, cry and punch himself. He new he loved Sonja more than anybody in the world. He never waited to find out why she was there nor where she was staying. He had heard about a benefit. So if she came for that what hotel was she staying in. Maybe she was sharing a room with someone, but whose name was it in and again, what hotel?

Tim wanted to call Deloris or Novadec, but he was ashamed. Maybe Sonja called them and told them what happen. Tim took the bus and w-n to the theater, hoping the cast maybe practicing.

Sonja wasn't there, but he hung around for a while. He knew a few of the people there. He managed to get a tenative list of the people that would be trying out. Sonja name was on the list. That was a plus for him. He knew, at least, she would be there until Sunday if she was picked. Tim went to work early. He wanted to get there before the other guys left because he wanted to get someone to work in his place that Saturday night.

Sonja figured Tim was still upset about Little Wayne or he had someone else. Little Wayne was killed almost six months ago and even she still felt a little bad about it. However, there was nothing she or anyone else could do about it now. She knew she still loved Tim very much. He had never spoke to her that way before. Tim had never raised his voice to her. She knew he wanted to be with her. Sure. wanted the same thing butt1-ming ·was all wrong. She had to deny him and herself. It would have been wrong to allow anything to happen. Someone had to be in control. Sonja had a very troubling sleep that night. She couldn't help but think about the time she spent ln Tim's arms today. She thought. I guess Tim was angry with me. I allowed him to hug and kiss me, on his bed, alone in the apartment and when he needed me, I pulled away. I didn't mean to lead him on. I was so happy to see him an be in his arms, I keep forgetting how easy he gets arroused sexually. I'll try to get the girk to come with me so I can apologize. I'll never go to his room alone again." All of them from the school got a part in the show. The following day Sonja was busy at the theater. They were getting everyone organized, with the order they would perform and getting used to the musicians. They did not leave the theater until late that evening. Everyone was so tired they stopped for dinner in the hotel and went up to bed. Everybody slept late that Saturday morning.

When Sonja got up, a note was under the door addressed to her. There was a very short message

"I am sorry Baby, Please forgive me. I love you very much. I'll see you later. TIM".

Happy. She was on pins and needles the rest of the day. Wondering when he would show up. Sonja still had not seen Tim when it was her turn. She sang *Indian Love Call* with one of the guys from her college. Then she sang another song alone. Then she stood on the sideline watching the others performances. Each performer would enter on one side and the performance they exit the other. Sonja was sitting down talking to some of the others about places they had performed when she heard them announced. "Timothy Leroy Coil will sing The Unreachable Stars." Her mouth open in astonishment. He beckoned for her to come on stage with him. Tim sang to her. She sang to him and then they ended by singing together.

Just about everybody could see and feel the love flowing between the two of them. Tim could barely wait to get Sonja off the stage before taking her in his arms. He had to force himself to let her go long enough to take another bow. After they had settled down, they talked.

Tim spoke first. "Baby, I am sorry."

Sonja responded, "Okay, I suppose I ask for that."

"Yes, you did, in a way, but just to let you know how I feel, we are going to get married no sooner than we can get the license, understand."

"Tim," cutting her off

"I don't want, nor will I except any opposition, any questions.?" Sonja was almost speechless, but she muddled something.

"Where will I be while we are waiting?" "At the hotel."

"But Tim."

"I don't want to hear it. I am not waiting wany longer. I want you to be my wife now."

81

"I must talk to my parents. You are talking about our life together, forever. Marriage is not only about sex. It's a lifetime of loving each other throughout eternity. Tim, I love you too, but this cannot happen tomorrow. Who is going to quite which college? How are we going to support ourselves? Where will we live? Let's continue to love each other enough to make plans."

"I hear what you are saying. Okay, let's go call our parents, to let them know what I want to happen now. You can also tell your roommates to leave without you."

"Tim, I do not have any clothing. I only brought a few things."

"That will be enough. If you need anything, I will purchase it." Sonja went up to the room to call her parents. then she also realizes, she had test schedules and papers to finish. She had to return to her college and he had to understand. She place the call and reverse to charges. Deloris felt that Sonja's choices of words were telling her that she really wanted to get married but not this minute. She told her his exact words and she knew they were not Sonja's words. One of the girls ask Tim a question and he walked over to where she was and that gave Sonja a chance to tell her mom that she had to get back to school because she had papers to complete and test to take. She didn't want to waste the semester. She was happy for her daughter, but she wanted to have some say in planning the wedding. After they talked for a while, she asks to speak to Tim.

"Hi, son-to-be." "Hi, Mom."

"I am very happy about the decision, but..." Tim thought, uh.uh, "Yes."

"Well, I need a favor." "Sure, anything." "Anything."

"Yes."

"It's a big favor."

"Will you stop holding me in suspense."

"Okay, if you are sure you want to know. You know I only have one daughter of my own and I have always wanted, if possible, for her to have a big wedding. Would it be too much to ask, if you two could wait until the semester ends? You only have about six weeks.

You both have to make plans for next semester. Where you are going to live and how will you support yourselves. Marriage is a big step. Please think about it for a moment. If you decide no, I will still love you as much as if you waited. However, I just thought I will ask. If you wait, we will have everything ready when you come. You can get married the day you set foot in town. If you have a free day before the semester ends, we will try you home to apply for your licenses. Now, what do you say.?"

All during the conversation Tim held onto Sonja. She couldn't imagine what her mother was saying because she was doing·all the talking. After she had got finished, Tim answered.

"Does Sonja know what you want and why?" "No."

"Well then, I have to talk to her." "You want to call me back.?"

"Yes, maybe that will be a good idea," Tim explained what transpired. Sonja left it up to him.

"Honey if that is what you want, it okay with me. You know you are a big help. However, your mother has some valid point If we get married right now, I certainly will not want you to leave me, nor do I think I would be in a concentrating mood to study for finals or do reports and I should not rob you of something you worked for all year. Gall your Mom and tell her we will wait."

Tim. before I call, I believe she would want us to tell her how we want things to go and who we want to participate in our wedding."

"I guess you are right. Just give her the go ahead and to call us with what she wants us to do." Tim hated to see Sonja leave, but Deloris was right. He wants more than anything for Sonja, Novadec and Deloris to be happy.

# CHAPTER 10

It was a short time to prepare for a wedding, but Deloris had everything in order. Novadec and the children were right there helping in everyway. In fact, Novadec's whole family got into the act. Wi- everyone helping thing begin to fall in place.

Sonja was the first to marry of the senior Felders grands.

She, also the first to really make the Felder family proud to be a Felder. Whenever any of the family were out somewhere, someone was sure to ask. "Are you related to Sonja Felder?"

They felt proud to say. "Yes, she is my Cousin, Niece, Grand, or Sister." What ever the case may be. Novadec's children loved her because she was so down-to-earth. When she would visit or they visit her, before Novadec and Deloris remarried, she would play the same games they did. She would eat the same foods, laugh at the same things they did and help clean up no matter if she was home or their house. Sonja never expects special treatment. When they went school shopping, Sonja bought clothing just like they did. They always forget that she was a celebrity.

Sonja had a couple parts in classical movies and was on TV a couple times. She was contacted for some other parts, but she turned them down. She preferred singing. The money she earned, Deloris banked it for her. She was far from spoiled. She and Deloris had a special mother- daughter relationship, as well as, true being friends. Every since, she could understand about life Deloris would explain why she did not want her to do or have certain things. Then she would allow her to decide whether she should go against her mother's will. Ninety percent of the time Sonja could not find a reason to do so. She would always confide in her mother about anything, she had questions about.

She was much the same with Novadec. On one occasion she ask Novadec why he stopped loving Deloris and left them and went to live with someone who drinks liquor, smoke cigarettes all the time, when her mom says it is wrong to do. "Daddy, how can you kiss her when her breath almost knocks you out." Novadec was embarrassed. She said, "My mommy never smells or looks like Nora.

Nora wants me to call her mommy. Daddy, she can't be my mommy can she Dad? She is just your wife Daddy. Right Daddy?" A statement like that coming from a young child shocked Novadec but, he had to find some answer for her. He couldn't tell her what a mistake he made and that he in love with Deloris. He started out attempting to answerher question but soon ventured off into an entirely different conversation which interest Sonja and took her mind off the real question she asked.

While Deloris and Novadec was reminiscing about their daughter and organizing the wedding they discuss many of her attributes and **innuenders** while she was growing up. Novadec felt at a lost for not being there for her. He kissed Deloris as he spoke.

"Baby? I am sorry? I wasn't here to help you. I wanted to be, especially when I found out how I goofed. I have never stopped loving you. It's just that, I was being pulled from all areas, away from you. When I found out what was happening, I was angry. My own parents, had no business pushing Nora on me by allowing her to sleep with me in the room we shared as husband and wife."

"Oh Novy, I suppose their opinion of me was quite low and I didn't fit in and neither did Sonja. The farm life was not us."

"I know Baby, believe me, I know. Oh, by the way, I have been planning on selling this house and buying a little farm

"What? Now Honey---." Novadec laughed and took Deloris in his arms. "I am only joking baby."

"Sure?"

"Sure enough." "I love you."

"Baby, you are mine forever."

Sonja was a beautiful bride. Nevadec was proud to walk her down the aisle but sad to let her go. To him, she was still his little girl. Wearing Deloris's wedding gown, he saw so much of her mother in her. That slightly oval shape face, with dark, thick eyebrow, long eye lashing over shadowing those medium big brown eyes which seem to penitrate right through you. Sonja had the type of face if someone who could never play the part of a mean or evil person. She looked and appeared to be sweet, thoughtless and innocent, but she was strong. She knew what direction she was going, and quite direct in her dealings with others. Never argue with anyone and will make a point and stick with it. She will let you think you are in control. She will cry and walk away with her head held high before allowing herself to become angry. She is a young woman of many things and to love her is to love her even more.

As she walked down the aisle, Tim wanted to go meet her. He wanted to hold her ih·hTsarmsforever. The three seat church filled to capacity, even the sidelines had chairs filled. As for Tim, he couldn't see anyone but Sonja. He did managed to say "I DO" and "I WILL" and followed along with some other questions and responses. When the Minister finally said "You may salute the bride." The minister had to tap him on the shoulder to complete the ceremony. Afterward, there was the picture taking and then the reception. He wished he could close his eyes and when they open, just he and Sonja would be there. Between Deloris and Mrs. Coil. about two hundred invitations was sent. They were not expecting all of them to come because they were sent about a week and a half before the wedding. Many people heard about the wedding and called. The family just told them where everything was going to be and didn't bother taking down names.

It was a good thing Deloris had selected a well prepared caterer because it was four hundred or more at the reception. They all came with nicely wrapped gifts or cards with money or gift cerificates.

Tim realized now he will have Sonja for an eternity. He could relax and enjoy the surrounding. After the picture taking, then greeting everyone at the reception, eating and mingling he refused to stay and open gifts. They Deloris all the cards to hold. All their things were taken over to Deloris house. They were driven there to change their clothing.

Tim's parents paid for a three day honeymoon and airfare so they only had a couple hours to catch their flight.

Deloris kept her house after she and Novadec got married. She wasn't sure why but she had a sneaky suspicion it would be occupied in the near future. She sort of felt they could not torture themselves by being apart for too much longer. Since both of them were struggling to finish their education and Sonja her singing. If they marry, they would need a place to live. Since her house was just about paid for she would give it to them.

When Sonja and Tim returned from their honeymoon, Deloris and Novadec told them while the family was there sorting through the wedding gifts so they could send thank you cards.

Seeing all the gifts, Tim spoke up.

"Honey, where are we going to store these gifts until we can afford a place?" Deloris responded. "Why don't you leave them at your house.?"

Tim smiled. "We don't have a place yet."

Deloris looked over at Novadec as he spoke. "Hey you guys, this is your house, if you want it and can pick up the mortage."

Tim and Sonja looked at each other in astonishment. Tim trying to talk, but but the word wouldn't come out right. "The ... th .. th .. our ... our .. ho .... hom .. but .. but."

"No buts, Deloris and I talked it over. It's our gift to you and my daughter. That's why she didn't get rid of it when we got married."

"We really thank you, but we still have a problem." "What is the problem?"

"Well, Sonja has another year and a half in college. My plans are to get a small place near her college until she finishes, then move back home. We probably could still pay the mortage until our money ran out, but I know if I can find a job which will enable me to pay a mortage, rent, and our tuition. I still have another half year. We also have to eat."

Mrs. Coil spoke. "Honey, our gift to you can be to assist with the mortgage,"

Deloris spoke. "Tim, you know, we had planned for Sonja to attend four years of college and we will still honor that."

Tim and Sonja were almost in tears. Sonja blurts out. "Moml we forgot about something." "What Sonja."

"The money in my savings. The last I checked, I had quite a bit." Turning to Tim she spoke. "All the years I have been performing, I wasn't allowed to spend the money I earned. Well, sometimes she let me use five or ten percent of it for special things and transportation. I may have close to a hundred thousand dollars."

They talked and made plans. After getting all the gifts cards organized with who gave what and their addresses everyone left. Tim and Sonja were still on cloud nine. They had a big house to themselves, a little money in the bank and two sets of parents right by their side.

After a couple of weeks of honeymooning and organizing things in the house, Tim's father had to take a business trip out of town; to the city where Sonja attends college. He asked them to ride with him. Tim could look around for a job and a place to stay. Sonja encouraged Tim to go with his father so they could have some time together. Tim wanted Sonja to come, but she decided not too. They would be leaving very early that morning and return very late that night. Tim reluctantly went with his father.

Sonja used the time to browse around town, going from one shop to another. While in one store someone taps her on the shoulder. She was holding a dress in front of her to see how it might look on her. She turned.

"Hi Sonja,"

"Wilma, how are you?"

"Okay, and congratulation on your marriage to Tim." "Thanks."

"I guess you two will become parents soon."

"Oh, No…not until I finish college and Tim get settled and finds a good job." "Oh, I thought you were already pregnant because every thing was so sudden." "Gosh, I never thought people would think that."

"Well, knowing Tim, as I do, among others, that's the talk of the town."

"Sorry to disappoint them, but they are all wrong. You are the first to know, so spread the word. Tim and I love each other very much and we wanted to be together as one."

"I am sure you two spent many nights together, so why the rush.?"

"No, we had never spent any nights together, for any reason especially not for sex, because I was totally against sex before marriage. It can cause too much pain. Such as, unwanted children, social disease, and other problems. If Tim had not excepted me the way I was and go along with my morals, we would not be married today."

"Are you trying to tell me Tim was your first and not until you two got married?" "That's right."

"That may have been alright for you, but who else was he messing around with?" "No one."

"Sure, sure."

"It's what I believe and he assured me of. Only he and God knows any different."

"Well, my dear. we need to talk about men. Did he ever tell you about how I got pregnant with Little Wayne.?"

"No, I never asked, anyway, that was between you and him.

"I know what you have to do to get pregnant. I wasn't born yesterday. Regardless of what anyone has to say, he loved that little boy and cared very much about him."

"And how did you feel about him?"

"Wilma believe me, If I had met him, not knowing who his parents were, I still would have loved him very much. I had very little contact with him, but as much as I did, I fell madly in love with him. I was so hurt when he got killed."

"I guess you, like many others, feel I was totally responsible for his death?" "Why would I feel that way?"

"Tim does."

"He seldom mentions Little Wayne. I know he was hurt real bad. He wanted 80 much to care for him."

"What do men know about rearing children.?"

"My father took full responsibility for caring for my sisters and brother." "Where was your mother?"

I thought... "Oh, my parents were divorced when I was four. He remarried and had three children. Then his wife did not want to care for them and took full charge."

"Was that your father who marched down the aisle with you?" "Yes, my Mom and Dad remarried."

"Really, after he dumped her, she remarried him? "Where are your half sisters and brother?"

"They live with them." "Why did they divorce?

"That is something you have to ask them. When I want to know something about someone, I go to the source. Never the person who knows them because gets the wrong inpression about people. They tend to say the wrong things. They tend to say what they think, not the actual truth. You ask me things about Tim if you really want to know, ask him. I can only speak for myself. You ask me did I think you were the blame for Little Wayne's death. You have to ask yourself. I never point my finger at anyone because there are four pointing back at me. As for me, I don't want to know about other people's business affairs, I don't have time for that, I have too much of my own to take care of."

"Oh. I didn't mean any harm, I am sorry." "Sorry for what?"

"How did you like being in the movies and on TV?"

"It was just a short term thing. It was okay, but not what I want to spend a lot of time doing." "They only offered you those few parts huh?"

"No, not really. I got offered several parts and turned them down." "Why did you choose opera?"

"Like everyone else I have my taste in music."

"It's almost lunch time. Would you like to get a bite to eat?"

Looking at her watch. "Oh, so it is, maybe another time, I have to meet my mother for lunch." "Okay, see you around." Wilma went her way and so did Sonja.

The first place Tim went in to ask about employment the employer wanted to hire him. He was a bit leary about the job, but it paid well until he could find something in a better enviroment. It would coincide with him taking classes and having time to be with Sonja. Also, the company, his Dad, had business with that day owned an apartment complex and rented to a lot of professional couples, some with family. Many were doctors who were doing their internship and had to move around a bit. Some were there for six months, a year and some times longer and some just for the semester. The man did not charge a lot of rents because he knew the people would care for his property like their own. There was never plumbing problems, such as, stopped up toilets or sinks, scribbling on the walls, things laying around which create bugs. No one ever left without paying what was due. He trusted people and wanted to help struggling students. He wasn't looking for big profits from the complex. The apartment Tim looked at had an eat in kitchen, nice size bedroom, a kin closet and a medium size livingroom. It would be ready in two weeks. Mr. Rankins was in the process of upgrading some piumbling and electrical work in several apartments on one side. All the units were spoken for and it was so that he had that one no one had called for yet. Tim told Mr. Rankins that as soon as he got home he would send him a check. He could have given the deposit right then and there, but he wanted to talk to Sonja. Also, the job would be starting in two weeks. He accomplished a lot in such a short time.

As soon as he got home he recapped the proceedings of the day with Sonja. She was in agreement with all that he accomplished that day. They would start packing the following week and decide what they needed to take. The apartment was furnished so they wouldn't need to worry about furniture, which was good. They had to purchase pillows and mattress covers.

When Sonja left Wilma, in the store, to met her mother for lunch. In the restaurant, they sat across from one of Tim's school mates whose name was Henry. He had gotten one of Sonja's classmates pregnant and they got married right away, even though, she was only sixteen, at the time. It was good to know that they were still together. When they saw Sonja, they came over to congratulate her. When Sonja saw their son she was speechless because he was the splitting image of Little Wayne. She thought back and realized she had seen Wilma and Henry together a lot during the school year before she left. She and Henry's wife left about the same time. She never saw any kind of intimate relationship going on between Wilma and Tim. Nor was Tim able to explain having any encounter with Wilma. It was just that they were out drinking and woke up nude in the bed with Wilma which was why he never fought against fatherhood. He and Wilma were just friends hanging out with the same crowd. When Tim came home that night, Sonja could hardly wait to tell him. The following day Tim called Henry to see if they could have lunch. He agreed and they met.

"Hi man, I am glad to see everything is working out."

"Yeah, it took a while, but I got my baby. I will be moving out near the college until she finishes."

"You wanted to talk to me about something?" "Yeah, Wilma."

"Okay, shoot, but there is nothing between us since she tried to breakup Susan and me by trying to tell me she was expecting my expecting my child."

"Sorry to disappoint you but she was and blamed it on me. She even took me to court. Because I didn't want to put the child through any unneccessary test, I accepted responsibilities and paid the support."

"Timothy, are you kidding me. How do you know it was mine?" Tim took out Little Wayne's picture. Henry gasped, "He looks just like my son, Kirk. Where is he now?"

"He's dead." "What happen?"

"Wilma hated the child and from what I understand, because of her lack of care, just as sure as I am sitting here, unintentually though, she caused his death by turning him loose on a busy street."

"Tim, I am sorry, I didn't know, I just never believed her. She lied so much, which is why I broke up with her. She was always in some other guy's face. I knew you guys were just friends. I sure wish you would have talk to me."

"What was I going to say? We got drunk one night and I woke up nude in the bed with her the next day. I couldn't remember messing around with anyone that night. Anyway, I tried to get the kid, but the courts were too slow.

After Tim had met with Henry, he was happy to finally find out the truth about Little Wayne. Tim was also pleased that he did what he did for him the little while he lived. He felt bad bout the way his mother let him die. He still could not understand why or how a person chooses to give birth to a child and hate it so much. What a pity.

Tim and Sonia had discussed parenthood before they got married, or I should say, Sonja sat tim down and discussed parenthood. They both agreed that they did not want children right away. Tim wanted to finish school and become gainfully employed and Sonja wanted to finish school and continue in her singing career for about eight years because she had to travel a lot. She felt that when she became less active and able to stay home, maybe, just teaching, she will start a family. Less demand will be on her because she wanted to be the mother and housewife that's required.

Tim and Sonja settled into their apartment and Tim started to work three days later. He worked three to four days weekly. After school had started, he had obligations he had to fulfil at his college in order to graduate the following semester. The Hockey games started up again at his college. Each week he flew out to the college for two and most times three days. He still had the same roommates so he didn't have to worry about a place to stay.

He didn't want to leave Sonja alone, but he had no choice. There were times when he came home and Sonja was leaving for a performance out of town. She only took jobs which did not interfere with her classes. She got paid well for doing something she liked and was good at. Tim was upset many times, but he had to hold his peace because they discouss her career prior to their marriage. Sonja told him point-blank that if her career were a problem for him she would rather not get married right away.

She said, "Tim, I do love you, but I have worked long and hard to do something I love doing and I am not going to give it up to become a housewife, if that is what you are asking."

"No, no, I will not ask you to do that. Sonja I don't want to live without you any longer."

"Tim, look, I don't just want to live with you. It's important that we understand the reason we want to be together and it must not be for sexual gratification only. It must be for all times and eternity. It must be for after this life we will find .each other. We must be sealed here. The Bible says that "WHAT WE SEAL ON EARTH WILL BE SEALED IN HEAVEN." When we marry, that is what I want for us, or whoever I marry."

"I love you Sonja and I promise that I will always be the head of our family and what you want will be what I want, for the both of us and our children."

"Don't worry. I have a well developed head as well and you will not have to make all the decisions alone."

Tim realized he had a well developed opinionated women who was going to do what she wanted at all cost, even at the cost of their relationship. But he had to deal with it because he was very much in love with her. She was a companion and a woman in all areas. Sonja was a good wife, cook. lover and their home were always neat and clean. She fulfiled all the duties of a wife and he was inclined to participate and loved it. Sonja made him feel important. She consulted him in all things by seeking his approval. If he seemed reluctant anything, she suggested she would shy away from it. If there was anything she really wanted, she would give him all the reasons they should have it and sooner are later he would agree they should have it. For example, when he started school, he felt it was cheaper to drive those eight hours alone, out to his college, but she gave him all the reasons he should just spend the extra money and fly for safety reasons. Driving over the highway, alone, may fall asleep, the car may breakdown, those long dark roads at night and how she would worry about him. Sonja cuddled up in Tim's arms while making her plea.

"Honey please, I don't want you on the road for eight hours alone, suppose this or that and she went on and on."

"But Baby, you know what it will cost."

"Yes, you are worth the investment, because I will worry, please fly." "Planes crash too you know."

"I know? I will worry a little less if you fly."

"But, when we went out the drive was not that bad."

"I know because I was with you and helped to drive when you got tired. When I and my friends drove out it was four of us, and when we got there, we were very tired."

"I will call the airline to see if I can concoct a student deal. It's worth a try." Sonja argued to point and won. Even though it would cost a little more monetarily Tims'mind was set at ease because he dreaded that long drive twice a week.

Tim graduated that following Fall with honors. He got a call from a major league hockey team to play Hockey, but he turned it down. He took a job where Sonja WQS finishing up her degree. He explained to the company that he would be temporary until his wife finishes college and they would not be relocating in that area. The company manager explain that they have a branch close to where they would be living and if he was interested he could be tranfered there, if everything works out. Tim took the job with that in mind.

A year later Sonja graduated. She was getting more involved with the Opera Company. They wanted her to go on tour. She was placed in some top lead roles which required her to be away sometimes for weeks. Tim was displeased regardless of what they agreed upon. Sonja understood and she decided to only involved herself in shows which may require her to be away for a day or two. Since most of the shows were on weekends, Tim would follow her after work on Fridays.

A lot of Tims' work was done on computers anyway. So he worked it out with his boss. Tim agrees for Sonja to go on a couple tours and he was with her all the way. He reaches a point where he was enjoying the traveling, the people they dealt with and some times he stood in for a few people who had a problem. He was always at the rehearsals, so he knew the parts.

When he return home, he went into the office and spent some time. Many times Sonja was asked to teach a class or give a talk at a school to promote the opera company in that area.She was always paid quite well. Most people in the area were aware of her accomplishments and had been following her career over the years. Each time Sonja gave a presentation the enrollment went up. Many people wanted that success for their children.

After seven years, Sonja began to decline offers which required her to be away too long and travel long distances.She cut back to four major performances a year and a couple TV specials.

Tim had been talking about children which were her reason for cutting back. Without Tim knowing she went to her doctor and told her, she was getting off birth control medicine and will trying to conceive. Physically she was fine and the doctor gave her the go ahead.

Three months after she found out she was expecting.

Sonja went to the store and bought a set of baby dishes. spoons and all. She made dinner and had the table set when Tim came home. When he saw the table setting, he cried...real tears. He was speechless. When he did, speak.

"Now I know why now I know why. I love you so much, I love you so much. My family is going to be complete. My family is going to be oomplete."

For the next eight month, he waited on Sonja hand and foot. He was forever on the telephone with his parents and Delores and Novadec. They answered the same questions over and over. Both their families were involved. Sonja's sister and brother came out and stayed with her a week and was forever on the telephone.

Their first child was a boy. Of course, they named him Timothy!!. Then carne a daughter. another son and another daughter.

Tim nor Sonja ever regret anything about their life. They both were very happy

Printed in the United States
by Baker & Taylor Publisher Services